Meet the

MADELEINE L'ENGLE

Meet the
Austins

SQUARE
FISH

Farrar, Straus and Giroux

SQUARE
FISH

An Imprint of Macmillan

MEET THE AUSTINS. Copyright © 1960 by Madeleine L'Engle, renewed 1988 by
Crosswicks, Ltd. Copyright © 1980, 1997 by Crosswicks, Ltd.
All rights reserved. Printed in the United States of America. For information,
address Square Fish, 175 Fifth Avenue, New York, N.Y. 10010.

Meet the Austins was first published in slightly different form in 1960
by The Vanguard Press, Inc.
The chapter entitled "The Anti-Muffins" was first published in slightly different form in 1980
by The Pilgrim Press.

Library of Congress Cataloging-in-Publication Data
L'Engle, Madeleine.
Meet the Austins / Madeleine L'Engle.
p.   cm.
Summary: The life of the Austin family is changed by the arrival of self-centered young
Maggy Hamilton, orphaned by the sudden death of her pilot father.
[1. Family life—Fiction. 2. Orphans—Fiction.]   I. Title.
PZ7.L5385Me   1997 [Fic]—dc20   96-27655

ISBN-13: 978-0-312-37931-5 ✓ ISBN-10: 0-312-37931-5

Square Fish and the Square Fish logo are trademarks of Macmillan and
are used by Farrar, Straus and Giroux under license from Macmillan.

Published in the United States in hardcover by Farrar, Straus and Giroux
Designed by Lilian Rosenstreich
Square Fish logo designed by Filomena Tuosto
First Square Fish Edition: September 2008
10 9 8 7 6 5 4 3 2 1
www.squarefishbooks.com

To my family

Contents

Introduction

"Who are you in this book?" we would constantly ask our grandmother, Madeleine L'Engle, about every book that she wrote. Her books have protagonists that many people can identify with, generation after generation, whether it is the brave and clever, gawky and frustrated Meg Murry, or the vulnerable and awkward, but at the same time, sensitive and intuitive Vicky Austin. Madeleine also strongly identified with her characters, and said many times that she was both Meg and Vicky. There was so much that was recognizable as her and her life in her stories, and we wanted to be able to map her fiction to her biography, thereby fixing and understanding her place, and by extension, ours, in the family and the wider world.

Most children want to be told stories about themselves. We were no different, and so, reading the Austin books was always a special thrill, because the narrative is peppered with incidents and details that also featured in family lore, like the adorable malapropisms of Rob Austin and Vicky's bicycle accident. The Austin family house in the quiet New England village of Thornhill (as described in *Meet the Austins*) is ever-present as a touchstone of their domestic peace, and is modeled on Crosswicks, a pre-Revolutionary War farmhouse in northwestern Connecticut where our grandparents and their children lived in the 1950s. The cross-country road trip in *The Moon by Night* copies the Franklin family itinerary of 1959, during which Madeleine started writing *A Wrinkle in Time*. In *The Young Unicorns*, the Austin kids unravel a mystery at the Cathedral of St. John the Divine, where our grandmother was the librarian and writer-in-residence for more than forty years.

There is enough similarity of detail in the books to have caused us some confusion: If our grandmother is Vicky, how can she have the bicycle accident that left our own mother with a Y-shaped scar on her chin? If some of the details confounded our sense of reality, we never questioned the underlying truth of the characters and our grandmother's relationship to them. If Madeleine were Vicky, then we felt understood. Because we were Vicky, too.

People would joke that *Meet the Austins* could have been called *Meet the Franklins* (Madeleine's married name), and yet, we knew that Vicky and the Austins couldn't be a simple translation of our grandmother's life, because of the family tension and pain surrounding these books about this family. Madeleine's own children were often shocked at how their own lives were appropriated and rewritten for publication, and felt judged against this very happy and practically perfect family. The line between fact and fiction can sometimes be blurry for writers, and the temptation to inscribe a certain version of and authority on events is strong.

All of Madeleine's writing, fiction and nonfiction, was an example of how all narrative is fiction, and all fiction can be true. She wrote and lectured extensively on the difference between truth and fact, arguing that it is through story that we human beings approach the truth, not through facts, which can only get us so far. As her granddaughters, this was both liberating and confusing, but we happily suspended our disbelief, and some of our best-loved stories are ones that are culled from her real life, from her days in the theater, from her early years with our grandfather, and the mysterious decade of the fifties.

The five books that are now presented as The Austin Family Chronicles were written over a period of thirty years. A prolific writer of more than sixty books in a variety of genres, Madeleine created a web of characters that grew, changed, and surprised her. As we re-read these books over our lifetime, what strike us are the very different responses we have to this family. At eleven, we thrilled to the references to things that our mother or aunt or uncle would confirm were true. At seventeen, we were cynical about the blur between fact and fiction, and thought we could read our grandmother as if she were a book. In our mature adulthood, we recognize how rich and complicated our grandmother was, and that fact can be the springboard for fiction, and fiction can inform who we are and tell us about ourselves.

Charlotte Jones Voiklis and Lena Roy
March, 2008

The Telephone Call

It started out to be a nice, normal, noisy evening. It was Saturday, and we were waiting for Daddy to come home for dinner. Usually he's home early Saturday, but this day he had a maternity case, and babies don't wait for office hours. Uncle Douglas was up for the weekend. He's Daddy's younger brother—ten years younger than Daddy—and he's an artist and lives in New York, and we all love him tremendously.

Mother had a standing rib roast cooking in the oven, because it's Uncle Douglas's favorite, and the kitchen smelled wonderful. Uncle Douglas and John were out in the old barn working on John's space suit, but the rest of us were in the kitchen. I don't suppose we're what you would call an enormous family, Mother and Daddy and the four of us children and the animals, but there are enough of us to make a good kind of sound and fury. Mother had music on, Brahms's *Second Piano Concerto*, kind of loud to drown us out. Suzy was performing an appendectomy on one of her dolls. She was doing this at the same time that she was scraping carrots, so the carrot scraper was a scalpel as well as a scraper.

Rob was supposed to be helping her, both with the appendectomy and the carrots, but he'd become bored, so he was on the floor with a battered wooden train making loud train noises, and Colette, our little gray French poodle, was barking at him and joining in the fun. Mr. Rochester, our Great Dane, was barking at one of the cats, who was trying to hide behind the refrigerator. I was being angelically quiet, but this was because I was doing homework—a whole batch of math problems. I was sitting near the fireplace and the fire was going and I was half baked (that's for sure, John would say) on one side, but I was much too cozy to move.

"Clamps," Suzy said loudly to an invisible operating-room nurse. "Retractors."

"Choo choo choo chuff chuff chuff," Rob grunted.

The Brahms came to an extra-loud part and everything was happy and noisy and comfortable.

Mother opened the oven door and poked at the potatoes roasting around the beef. "Vicky," she said, "why don't you go somewhere a little quieter to finish your homework?"

"Do I have to?" I asked.

"It's up to you," Mother said. "Suzy and Rob, please keep it down to a quiet roar."

Then the telephone rang.

Heaven knows, with Daddy being a doctor, we're used to the telephone. It rings all night as well as all day. We have two separate phone numbers, and when you call one it rings only at home, and when you call the other it rings both in Daddy's office and at home. John and I are the only ones allowed to answer the office phone, but when it's the house phone the younger ones run for it, too.

This was the house phone, and Suzy dropped her doll in the middle of the operation and ran. Rob shrieked, "It's my turn! I'll get it!" It really was his turn, but Suzy kept on running and Rob shrieked louder, especially because she got to the phone before he did. Mother turned down the volume on the record player and shouted at Mr. Rochester to stop barking and told Rob that he could answer next time, and Suzy said in a breathless voice, "Hello, this is Suzy Austin, who is this, please?" There was a moment's silence; then she said, more loudly, "But who is speaking, please?" and then she held the receiver out to Mother, saying, "Mother, it's for you, and I don't know who it is. I thought it was Aunt Elena but she didn't say hello to me or anything, so it couldn't be."

Mother went to the phone and I put my math book down on the floor and Mother glared at me and said, "Be quiet, Vicky!" as though I were hammering or something, and I knew something was wrong.

Then Mother said, "Oh, Elena, oh no!" and it was the strangest thing, looking at her, to see her get white beneath her summer brown. And then she said, "What can we do?" and then she was quiet for a long time, and then she said, "Oh, Elena, darling—" as though she were going to say something more, but she didn't say anything more, and then she hung up.

She stood there by the phone without saying anything, and Suzy said, "Mother, what is it? What is it?" and Mr. Rochester began to growl, and Rob said, in the terribly serious voice he gets when he thinks something important is going on, "Mr. Rochester, I think you'd better be quiet."

Mother said, "Vicky, go get Doug."

It wasn't dark yet, because we were still on daylight saving, but it was cold, windy cold, the way it gets around the time of the first frosts, and I ran across the brittle grass to the barn, shivering; I wasn't sure whether I was shivering because I was cold or because something awful had happened.

When I got to the barn John was in the space suit. He and Uncle Douglas had been working on it ever since last Christmas, when Uncle Douglas was up. It has a space-band radio, and a tank of oxygen and something-or-other mix, and in the helmet are all kinds of controls for the radio and air and heat and drinking water and even aspirin, because that was the only kind of pill Daddy would let John have. John spends every penny of his allowance on his space suit, and every penny he can earn mowing lawns or chopping wood or even baby-sitting if nothing else is available, and I'm sure Uncle Douglas slips him extras, though he's not supposed to, for things like the rubber gaskets John said he absolutely had to have. It's quite a space suit, and it won first prize for the state at the Science Fair.

They were so busy they didn't hear me, John in the helmet and Uncle Douglas wearing earphones. I knew the kind of thing they were saying: "Firefly calling Little Bear. Come in, Little Bear." And: "Little Bear to Firefly, shift to directional frequency at two centimeters." I pulled Uncle Douglas's sleeve.

He kind of brushed me away. "Just a minute, Vicky."

I pulled harder. "Uncle Douglas! Please!" I knew they couldn't hear me, but I babbled on, "Mother wants you right away. Aunt Elena called and I think something bad's happened."

Uncle Douglas must have seen by my face that I wasn't just interrupting them to invite them in for a cup of tea. He pulled off his earphones. "What?"

I told him again.

He spoke through the mike to John, told me to wait till John got out of the space suit, and ran out of the barn and across the lawn.

It takes John a good five minutes to get either in or out of his space suit. He lifted off his helmet and put it carefully on its shelf. "What's happened, Vic?" he asked me.

"I don't know," I said. "Aunt Elena called. And then Mother sent me out to get Uncle Douglas."

We didn't say anything else in all the minutes it took John to get out of his space suit. We were both afraid of the same thing. If Aunt Elena called, and it was something bad—and I knew that it was something bad—it must be about Uncle Hal.

Aunt Elena and Uncle Hal aren't our real aunt and uncle, but we love them as though they were. Aunt Elena was Mother's roommate at school in Switzerland and they've been best friends ever since. Aunt Elena is a concert pianist, and she plays all over the country and in Europe, too. Uncle Hal, her husband, is a jet pilot.

Now, we all knew Uncle Hal's work was dangerous, but he was so tremendously alive you couldn't imagine anything ever happening to him. He wasn't nearly as tall as Daddy, but he was sort of big and solid, like a rock, with a great booming laugh and brown eyes that twinkled and crinkled. He was one of the first pilots to go through the sound barrier, and whenever a new experimental plane was being invented, you knew Uncle Hal was going to be one of the first to fly it.

I stood there in the deepening shadows of the barn while John got out of his space suit, saying over and over to myself, Oh, God, please, please, make it be something else, not Uncle Hal, oh, please don't make it be anything awful.

Then, at last, John was out of his space suit. He said, "C'mon, Vic," and we went across the lawn to the house. It was just beginning to get dark, and the windows of the house were blank and empty, and no one turned on a light inside.

We went into the kitchen and Mother was still standing by the phone in her blue-and-white-striped cotton dress and I could see that she was trembling, and I was afraid. Usually, whatever happens, Mother can make it safe again, but whatever this was, I knew there was nothing she could do to make it all right. She put her hand up to her forehead as though to smooth back her hair, but her hair was quite tidy. She said— and her voice sounded like somebody else's voice entirely— "Uncle Hal had an accident with his plane today. He was killed instantly."

I looked at Uncle Douglas and he looked angry, as though he wanted to swear, as though he wanted to stamp around, as though he wanted to hit somebody. But all he did was sit down and glare into the fire.

Mother said, "Vicky, take Rob upstairs and give him a bath and put him in his pajamas before Daddy comes home."

Suzy said, "But we were all going star—"

John said, "Suzy!"

But Mother just said, in that funny quiet voice she uses only when she's very angry or very upset, "Not tonight, Suzy. Go on up and get into your nightclothes. All of you. You, too, John, please."

John is the oldest and wisest of us, and I think he knew that Mother wanted terribly to be able to call Daddy, and all I wanted in the world was to have Daddy come home, to feel him put his arms around me and give me a tight hug and know that he was all right. As I started upstairs with Rob I saw John put his arms around Mother, and I realized suddenly how he must have shot up during the summer, because as he stood there by her he was as tall as she is, and we are a tall family. His face was very grave, and he looked almost grown up as he gave Mother a hug, and then he turned and came upstairs, too, but slowly, not three at a time, his usual way.

I ran Rob's bath and let him put in all his bath toys, which meant that there was scarcely any room for Rob, since he has all kinds of things for bath toys as well as the usual ducks and boats. He has a sand bucket and an old telescope and a bent muffin pan. He played noisily, and I had an awful time trying to keep him from splashing water all over the bathroom floor, and I was angry because I didn't think he cared or understood about Uncle Hal at all.

John and Suzy were absolutely quiet getting ready for bed; the whole house sounded like another place, not like our house at that time of day. I just sat on the toilet lid and watched Rob and told him to wash his knees, and he wouldn't wash his face with soap, so I did it for him, and then he started to yell and scream and I was sure I hadn't got any soap in his eyes; I'd been especially careful. Then John came in and shouted at me, for heaven's sake, couldn't I think of Mother for once and do a simple thing like giving Rob his bath without causing all this sound and fury?

I sat back down again and I started to shout at John, but, instead, my voice sort of crumpled and I said, "Oh, John."

He said, "I'm sorry, Vic," and went out, buttoning the top of his brown-and-white-striped pajamas. Colette, our French poodle, lay on the bath mat and waited for Rob to get out of the tub so she could lick his feet, and Rob giggled at her when she did it, as though nothing had happened at all. And I wanted to shake him.

I got Rob's pajamas on him and took him in Suzy's and my room and sat him down on my bed while I got into my own nightclothes. Colette scrambled up on the bed by him. I think both Mr. Rochester and Colette are particularly fond of Rob because he's such a baby—he's almost five years younger than Suzy—and he loves them so, he's always hugging them and kissing them. When he was a baby he used to ride Mr. Rochester as though he were a horse, and sometimes Mr. Rochester will still let him do it.

Suzy had taken off her clothes but she hadn't done anything else. She stood there, naked except for a bandage on her knee where she'd skinned it, and scribbled on the blackboard with a scrap of yellow chalk, and I said, "Suzy, you'll catch cold and Mother'll be furious," and she turned away from the blackboard as though I'd woken her up in the middle of a dream.

We heard Daddy coming in. The back door slammed and

12

we heard him call out to Mother, but we didn't go tearing down the stairs and dash at him the way we usually do. Suzy sat on the floor pulling on her slippers and I tied the belt to my bathrobe three times, and John came in and said, "Everybody ready?" Rob put up his arms to be carried, as though he were still a baby, and John picked him up and said, "Well, I think Daddy's home," and we all crept downstairs.

Daddy was standing in the kitchen with his arms around Mother and neither of them was saying anything, but for just a moment everything seemed safe and all right again; and then Daddy saw us and said, "Well, children," and dropped his arms, and Mother said, "We'd better eat dinner. Call Douglas, please, Wallace." Daddy called and Uncle Douglas came in from the study, still looking terribly angry.

We sat down and said grace, but saying thank you, even for food, seemed a strange thing to do. And not one of us tasted the roast beef or any of the other special things Mother had fixed for Uncle Douglas. It might have been sawdust.

I took up a mouthful and tried to chew it, and when I looked over at Daddy my heart ached with love and fear. Uncle Hal was dead, and so, suddenly, Daddy was in danger, too; and I looked at him and thought how very terribly I loved him, every part of him, and then I noticed all kinds of things about him that I'd just taken for granted or hadn't seen before. There was quite a lot of gray in his nice brown hair, more than I remembered being there, and his forehead seemed higher, too. And there were some new gray hairs in his bristly eyebrows. He sat there eating, grave, but not sort of stricken like the rest of us. He saw me looking over at him, and he looked up at me and his brown eyes, with sort of golden flecks in them, smiled at me, and somehow I felt better.

After dinner Uncle Douglas took Suzy and Rob into the study and played with them, and John and I helped Mother and Daddy put the dishes in the dishwasher and clean up, and before we'd finished Daddy got a call and had to go down to the hospital. He put his arms around Mother again and said, "I don't think I'll be very long. I'll be home as soon as I can and I'll phone you if I'm longer than I expect." Then he kissed us all good night and slung Rob over his shoulders like a sack of flour and took him upstairs and dumped him down on his bed.

Mother came up to read to us and put us to bed. We were in the middle of *The Jungle Book* then. We always try to pick things everybody will like for the read-aloud books, and even Rob enjoyed Mowgli and Rikki-tikki-tavi. But Mother only read us a couple of pages. We were in Suzy's and my room. We take turns: one night Suzy's and my room, the next night John and Rob's. There are twin beds in Suzy's and my room, and John sat on the foot of Suzy's bed, and Rob got in with me and messed all the bedclothes up, and Mother sat on the floor between the beds. Colette curled up cozily in Mother's lap and yawned all through the reading. Mr. Rochester very seldom comes upstairs; Mother and Daddy don't encourage it, he's so big. But that night he didn't seem to want to stay downstairs; he must have sensed that something was wrong, so we heard him lumbering up. Poor Rochester, he's very heavy on his feet, and clumsy, too, and he's always getting scolded for bumping into things and knocking them over. It's very sad for him, be-

14

cause Colette's so delicate and graceful. Now Mr. Rochester sniffed around both beds and finally sat down with a thud by Mother and Colette.

When Mother closed the book, we turned out the light and said prayers. We have a couple of family prayers and Our Father and then we each say our own God Bless. Rob is very personal about his God Bless. He puts in anything he feels like, and Mother and Daddy had to scold Suzy to stop her from teasing him about it. Last Christmas, for instance, in the middle of his God Bless, he said, "Oh, and God bless Santa Claus, and bless you, too, God." So I guess that night we were all waiting for him to say something about Uncle Hal. I was afraid maybe he wouldn't, and I wanted him to, badly.

"God bless Mother and Daddy and John and Vicky and Suzy," he said, "and Mr. Rochester and Colette and Grandfather and all the cats and Uncle Douglas and Aunt Elena and Uncle Hal and . . ." and then he stopped and said, "and all the cats and Uncle Douglas and Aunt Elena and Uncle Hal," and then he stopped again and said, "and especially Uncle Hal, God, and make his plane have taken him to another planet to live so he's all right because you can do that, God, John says you can, and we all want him to be all right, because we love him, and God bless me and make me a good boy. Amen."

Mother didn't sing to us that night. She usually sings to us, but she said, "I'm going downstairs now, children. Please be good and try to go to sleep right away. Run along into your own room, John and Rob. I'll come tuck you in as soon as I tuck in the girls."

Rob slowly got out of my bed. He stood up on the foot of it and said to Mother, "Do you ever cry?"

"Of course, Rob," Mother said. "I cry just like anybody else."

"But I never see you cry," Rob said.

"Mothers have to try not to cry," Mother said. "At least, not too often. Now, run along to your own room."

She tucked Suzy and me in, and kissed us, and then we heard her go in to Rob and John.

I couldn't go to sleep. I lay there and my bed was all rumpled up from Rob, and I got up and straightened it out and tucked it in again and lay there on my back and I couldn't sleep. I whispered, "Suzy," but she didn't answer. She only sighed heavily and turned over and I knew that she was asleep. I was cold, and Mother hadn't put on our winter blankets yet, and I pulled up the bedspread and lay there with the covers under my chin, and it wasn't only because autumn was coming that I was cold.

Suzy's and my room is over the study, and I could hear Mother and Uncle Douglas talking, just the rumble of their voices, Uncle Douglas's deep and rich, Mother's lighter. Then the phone rang and then there was silence for a long time, and then their voices again, and then another phone call. Suzy's little blue clock seemed to tick louder and louder, and finally I put on the light to see what time it was, and it was after eleven.

I couldn't stand it any longer. I got up. I went to the bathroom, and then I looked into John and Rob's room, but they were both asleep. I'd been hoping John would be awake, too, because I knew that he felt worse about Uncle Hal than any of the rest of us.

I went and sat for a moment at the top of the back stairs,

because the light and warmth from the kitchen came up to me and gave me a feeling of safety. Then I heard Mother on the telephone: "Yes, of course, Douglas will drive right down; wait a minute, Elena, I'll put him on."

I knew that I mustn't eavesdrop, but I couldn't go back upstairs and to bed, so I went on down. Uncle Douglas must have been right by Mother, because he was holding the phone to his ear, and Mother saw me and said, "Vicky," and then, "Go wait in the study." In a moment she came and joined me, saying, "What's the matter, Vic?"

"I couldn't sleep."

She nodded. "I know. How about the others?"

"I think they're all asleep."

"John?"

"He's asleep. Mother," I started. "*Why? Why* did Uncle Hal have to be——"

But then Uncle Douglas came in. "Vic," he started to say to Mother; then he saw me. "Oh, hello, Vicky, what are you doing?"

"She was just wakeful," Mother said quickly for me. "So now what, Doug? Are you going?"

"Yes," Uncle Douglas said. "Right away."

"Where's Uncle Douglas going?" I asked. I was all tangled up in my mind, because it didn't seem fair for Uncle Douglas to be dashing off again just after he had come. We all loved him so terribly much, and I hadn't had a chance to see him at all, really, since he'd arrived the night before, and yet I didn't understand how I could be disappointed about a thing like that at a time like this.

17

He came over to me and put his hand under my chin so that he could look down into my eyes. I looked up at him, hoping that he could straighten me out, because, though Uncle Douglas is always making jokes and people call him a bohemian because he's an artist and maybe because of his beard, too, he also seems able to straighten things out. He says it's because he's not around all the time, so he has perspective on us.

Now he said, "Aunt Elena needs me, little one. I'm going to see if I can be of any help to her. She's very much alone now. And Uncle Hal's copilot was killed, too, you see, and he had a little girl. She doesn't have any mother, so your Aunt Elena's in charge of her for the moment. So that's another complication, too."

"Oh," I said, and it all seemed more frightening and terrible than ever.

"Go upstairs now, Vicky," Mother said. "Try to go to sleep or you'll never be up in time for Sunday school tomorrow. I'll come up to you later and see if you're still awake."

Uncle Douglas kissed me goodbye, his beard tickling me softly, and I trailed on upstairs. I climbed into bed and the night-light from the bathroom came in gently, and by and by a rectangle of light came in through the window and wheeled across the ceiling, and it was Uncle Douglas getting his car out and driving off.

Because I knew that Mother would come in to me, I was able to relax a little as I lay there, instead of just bouncing around the way I'd been doing before. I didn't want to sleep. All I wanted to do was to talk, to talk to people who were alive and who could help make me less frightened and confused. I don't know exactly why I was so frightened and confused; maybe if I'd known why, I wouldn't have been.

I heard Daddy come home, and then he and Mother came upstairs. I heard Daddy take Rob to the bathroom, and then Mother came in to me and sat down on the side of my bed, and the light from her bedside lamp shone across the hall and onto my bed and her face.

"Mother, how old is the little girl?" I asked.

She must have been thinking very hard about something else, because she said, "What little girl?"

"The one whose father was Uncle Hal's copilot."

"Ten."

A year older than Suzy; two years younger than I am. And she didn't have a mother or a father. "Mother, I don't understand life and death."

Mother laughed softly, a little sadly, and ran her hand over my forehead. "My darling, if you did you'd know more than anybody in the world. We mustn't talk any more now. We'll wake Suzy."

And Daddy came and stood in the doorway, saying quietly, "Vicky, John is asleep and you must try to go to sleep, too."

He and Mother went into their room and turned off their light, and the soft sound of their voices talking quietly together must have acted like a lullaby on me, because I turned over and went to sleep.

Sometime during the night the phone rang again; I woke up just enough to realize it. And it rang again in the morning—the house phone both times, not the office ring; but once I had finally gone to sleep I was so sleepy that the sound of the phone hardly got through to me, and it was only as I was waking up, with the sun shining full across my bed, and heard the office phone ringing that I remembered the phone had rung during the night.

We have lots more time on Sundays than we do on school-days, but there always seems to be more of a rush to get to Sunday school on time than there is to catch the school bus, so we don't make our beds till we get home from Sunday school and church. As soon as we got home from church Mother told us to get out of our good clothes and into play clothes (I don't know why we'd never do it if she didn't tell us, but there's always so much to do that we just don't think about it) and then she told me to strip my bed and make it up with clean sheets. "And check the guest room, Vicky," she said. "Make sure there are clean sheets on the guest-room beds."

"Why?" I asked.

"Because I tell you to," she said, as though I were Rob, and that was all.

I was almost through when she came up and said, "Vicky, would you mind sleeping in Rob's room for a while?"

"Me? Why?" I asked in surprise.

"You must have realized that Aunt Elena called several times last night. I talked with her again this morning, and Uncle Douglas is driving her up here with Maggy."

"Maggy?"

"Margaret Hamilton, the little girl whose father was Uncle Hal's copilot."

I hadn't quite finished making the bed, but I sat down on the edge of it. "When are they coming?"

"They're on their way now," Mother said. "They ought to be here this afternoon. I thought that since Maggy and Suzy are so close in age, I'd put Maggy in your bed."

"What about John?"

"He'll sleep in the study tonight while Aunt Elena's here. When she goes, he can have the guest room. I know you have a lot of homework this year, Vicky, but John has even more, and I think he must be the one to have the room to himself. It won't be all gravy, you know; he'll have to move out whenever we have company."

I thought this over for a moment. Then I said, "How long is the little girl . . . Maggy . . . staying?"

"I don't know," Mother said. "We'll just have to see."

"And Mother . . . why is she coming to us?"

"It's too complicated to go into now," Mother said briskly. "Come along, Vic, let's get the beds done."

Mother usually gives us nice, full explanations for things, but on the rare occasions when she doesn't (I think being cryptic is what I mean), there's no point asking any more questions, so we just finished up with the beds.

After lunch John had to work on his science project, so he went off to the barn, with Daddy warning him to do his project and not his space suit. I biked over to the center of Thornhill to check my math homework with Nanny Jenkins, my best friend. Nanny's parents run the store in the village and Mr. Jenkins plays the cello, too. Math is not my best subject and I find that if

I don't check my problems I'm apt to make silly mistakes in adding or subtracting that make the whole problem wrong even if I've been doing it the right way. We finished about five o'clock and it was time for me to get along home, anyhow. Mother doesn't like us to ride our bikes after dark unless there's a very good reason. It's a nice ride home from the village, up the one real street in Thornhill, a nice wide street with white houses set back on sloping lawns and lots of elms and maples (it's just a typical New England village—at least, that's what Uncle Douglas says), and then off onto the back road. The back road is a dirt road, and it's windy and hilly and roundabout and so bumpy that cars don't drive on it very often. Our house is at the other end of it, just about a mile and a half. In the autumn it's especially beautiful, with the leaves turned and the ground slowly being carpeted with them. Where the trees are the heaviest and the road cuts through a little wood, the leaves are the last to turn, so that as I pedaled along, the evening sun was shining through green, and up ahead of me, where the trees thinned out, everything was red and orange and yellow.

A little green snake wriggled across the road in front of me, and I thought how thrilled Rob would be if he were along. Almost every day all summer he would go up the lane hunting for a turtle to bring home as a pet. We never found a turtle, but we've seen lots of deer, and a woodchuck that lives in the old stone wall by the brook, and any number of rabbits; and once we saw a red fox.

When I got home, Uncle Douglas's red car was parked outside the garage behind our station wagon, so I knew they were there.

And suddenly I felt very funny about going in, and took twice as long as I needed to put my bike in the shed. I hung my jacket up in the back-hall closet and picked up Suzy's and Rob's jackets, which they'd evidently hung on the floor, and put them on hangers—anything to put off opening the back door and going into the kitchen.

Why was I so shy about seeing Aunt Elena and meeting Maggy, or even saying hello to Uncle Douglas again when I'd been talking with him only the night before?

Finally there was nothing to do except open the door and go in, so I did. And instead of finding the kitchen full of everybody as it usually is at that time of day, I saw Aunt Elena standing in front of the stove alone. She turned to greet me and she said immediately and briskly, "Ah, Vicky, you've saved me. I am not ten feet tall like your mother and I cannot reach the coffee."

So I didn't have to say anything. I didn't even have to kiss her, which would have been the easiest thing in the world to do up to the time the telephone rang the day before and which now seemed to take more courage than I possessed. I pulled a stool over to the stove and climbed up on it and got the can of coffee.

"No, the other one," Aunt Elena said. "I promised your mother I'd make some café espresso for after dinner."

And all I could say was, "Oh." I stood there, watching her. She didn't look any different; she looked just the same way she had a few weeks before, when she and Uncle Hal were up for the weekend; and yet she wasn't the same person at all. She stood there in her black dress measuring coffee, wearing black not because of Uncle Hal but because she is a city person and she looks beautiful in black and wears it a great deal. Her hair is black, too, and in one portrait Uncle Douglas painted of her he used great enormous globs of blue and green in the hair, and, funnily enough, when it was done it was exactly right. We have a lovely portrait of Mother Uncle Douglas painted, and he's painted quite a few others of her, too, and one is in a museum. Uncle Douglas says he paints only beautiful women. But, he says, beautiful is not pretty. I don't really know whether Mother is beautiful or not. To me she looks exactly the way a mother should look, but only in the portrait where she's holding Rob just a few weeks after he was born does Uncle Douglas see her the way I do.

Aunt Elena doesn't look like a mother at all—and, of course, she isn't. Her black hair falls loose to her shoulders and she always looks to us as though she were dressed to go to a party. When she plays with us we always have a wonderful time, but it's as though we were brand new to her each time, not as though she were used to being around children at all. Uncle Hal, with his big booming laugh and the way he could roughhouse with us all, was quite different. I thought of Uncle Hal and remembered that I would never see him again, and I looked at Aunt Elena, and it was as though it were terribly cold and my sorrow was freezing inside me so that I couldn't speak.

John came in just then, bursting in through the kitchen door with his jacket still on and his face so pink from the cold that the lenses of his glasses began to steam up from the warmth of the kitchen.

24

John and I fight a lot, but I have to admit that John is the nicest one of us all. He seems to know what to do and say to people without having to think about it, and whenever there are elections and things John always gets elected president. So now he was able to do what I wanted to do and knew I ought to do and simply couldn't do. He went right up to Aunt Elena and put his arms around her and hugged her hard and kissed her. He didn't say anything about Uncle Hal, but it was perfectly obvious exactly what he was saying. For a moment Aunt Elena sort of clung to him, and then, just as I thought maybe she was going to start to cry, John took his arms away and said, "Aunt Elena, you're the only person around here who can untie knots, and my shoelace is all fouled up. Could you untie it for me?" And he yanked off his shoe and handed it to her.

Now, I am very good at untying knots and I always untie John's knots for him and I started to say so, indignantly, but then I realized what John was doing and I shut my mouth, just in time. Aunt Elena bent over John's shoe, and the tears that had been starting in her eyes went back, and when she handed John the shoe she smiled and looked like herself.

"Where's everybody?" John demanded.

"Your mother's out picking carrots," Aunt Elena said.

"Oh, no, not carrots again." John groaned. "I wish Rob had never planted those carrots. Where're the kids?"

"Your Uncle Douglas took them for a walk."

"What's for dinner—other than carrots? Carrot sticks this time, I hope. We had 'em cooked last night." He went over to the stove, lifted the lid off a big saucepan, and sniffed. "Um, spaghetti. Garlic bread?"

"But of course," Aunt Elena said as Mother came in, her arms full of carrots.

I was helping Mother scrape the carrots when there came the sounds of shouting and talking and then in they came, seeming like a whole horde of children instead of just three and Uncle Douglas.

And a dark-haired little girl came dancing in, screaming shrilly, "You can't catch me! You can't catch me!" and went dancing around the table, Suzy and Rob after her, and, of course, Rochester came dashing in to see what was going on and knocked over a chair, and the little girl knocked over another chair, not because she was clumsy, like Rochester and me, but because she wanted to hear the crash.

"All right," Mother said, far more pleasantly than she would have if it had been just us or one of our friends from around here, "this furniture has to last us for quite a long while. Let's keep the rougher kind of roughhousing for outdoors, shall we?"

And the little girl paid absolutely no attention. "C'mon, Suzy, chase me!" she shrieked, and knocked over another chair.

Mother's voice was still pleasant but considerably firmer. "Maggy, I said not in here, please. Suzy and Rob, pick up the chairs. Maggy, you haven't met John and Vicky yet. John and Vic, this is Margaret Hamilton."

John shook hands with her and said, "We're glad you've come to stay with us for a while, Maggy."

Maggy looked him up and down and said, "Well, I don't know if I'll like living way out in the country," in a sort of a disapproving way.

I shook hands with her and she looked me up and down in

the same way she had John and said, "You're not as pretty as Suzy."

Now, this is true, but it wasn't very tactful. Suzy is pretty and fluffy and she has curly blond hair, and I'm tall and skinny and my hair is sort of mousy and doesn't have any curl at all and I cut off my braids when I went back to school this autumn and I wish I hadn't. I know all this about myself, but I still got kind of red and unhappy when Maggy said that about Suzy and me.

Uncle Douglas said quickly, "Remember the story of the ugly duckling, Maggy? Vicky's going to be the swan of you all. Someday I'm going to paint her."

I could see that Maggy didn't like that very much, because she flounced over to Suzy, saying, "C'mon, let's go up to our room and play." Even when she flounced she was graceful, sort of like a butterfly, and if you hadn't known she wasn't Aunt Elena's daughter or any relation at all you would have thought Aunt Elena was her mother, because Maggy has the same shiny soft black hair and enormous dark eyes. Well, I guess that's really all that's alike, because under the flesh the bones are shaped differently. Aunt Elena's features are strong and definite, and her nose has a high bridge. And Maggy's face is soft and wistful, and her eyes are just a tiny bit almond-shaped.

She and Suzy started to dash upstairs and Mother called Suzy back down and told her to set the table first, and that from now on Maggy could help her.

"I don't know how," Maggy said flatly.

"Suzy will show you."

"Sure," Suzy said. "Come on, Maggy. How many tonight?"

"Count," Mother said automatically.

"Six of us," Suzy said, "and Maggy and Aunt Elena and Uncle Douglas is . . . is . . ."

"Seventeen," Rob said.

"Nine," Suzy said. "So we'll have to put the leaves in the table."

John went to get the leaves, because they're quite heavy, and there was a frantic scratching and a shrill barking, and Rochester bounded to the door, and we realized that Colette had been left out.

"I'll let her in," I said. "I'll be back in just a minute." Usually, just before dinner is the nicest time of day, but this evening I suddenly wanted to be alone for a few minutes. Was it just because Maggy had reminded me that I am plain? Mother says that I'm getting very broody, and part of it is my age, and most of it is just me.

I walked slowly around the house, with Colette prancing about me. It was nearly dark and lights were on in almost all the windows of the house and rectangles of light poured out onto the lawn. There were still a few leftover summer noises—a frog or an insect—and the air was clear and cold, and finally I had to run to keep warm and Colette began yipping and nipping at my heels in excitement, thinking I was playing a game just especially for her.

Then there came the sound of the piano, coming clear and beautiful out into the night, and I knew that Aunt Elena must be in the living room, playing. When she's with us she often sits at the piano and plays and plays and plays, but somehow I hadn't expected her to this time, and it made me feel more the crying kind of unhappy than I'd felt since the phone call. It wasn't that she was playing anything sad or anything——mostly it was Bach, I think——but just having her sit there at the piano, playing, and knowing that Uncle Hal would never hear her again made me want to go find Mother and put my head against her and howl.

I stayed out, listening for a moment, and when I went back in the house things had calmed down considerably. Aunt Elena was still at the piano; Suzy and Maggy must have gone upstairs; Rob and Uncle Douglas were watching television in the study; and John and Mother were talking while Mother made the salad.

"Vicky," Mother said, "tell Rob he hasn't put the napkins on the table yet and to come do it as soon as there's an ad on." Putting on the napkins and the table mats, when we don't use a tablecloth, is Rob's part of setting the table. Suzy does the silver and I do the china and glasses.

I went in to tell Rob, and when he'd gone into the kitchen to do his job I sat down on the arm of Uncle Douglas's chair.

"Turn that thing down, Vicky," he said. "It's blasting my ears off."

I turned down the volume and then went and sat by Uncle Douglas again. "What's on your mind, young lady?" he asked me.

I did have something on my mind; I did want to talk to him; how did he always know? "Uncle Douglas," I said, "why is it that John can show Aunt Elena he's sorry about Uncle Hal and I can't, and I'm so terribly, terribly sorry?"

Uncle Douglas put his arm around me and his beard rubbed gently against my cheek. "Aunt Elena knows you're sorry, dear."

, "But why does John know what to say, and how to say it, and all I can do is act stupid, as though it didn't matter?"

"Just because it matters too much. Have you ever heard of *empathy*?"

I shook my head.

"John can show Aunt Elena how sorry he is because he has a scientific mind and he can see what has happened from the outside. All good scientists have to know how to be observers. He can be deeply upset about Uncle Hal and deeply sorry for Aunt Elena, but he can be objective about it. You can't."

"Why?"

"Because you have an artistic temperament, Vicky, and I've never seen you be objective about anything yet. When you think about Aunt Elena and how she must be feeling right now, it is for the moment as though you *were* Aunt Elena; you get right inside her suffering, and it becomes your suffering, too. That's empathy, and it's something all artists are afflicted with."

"Are you?"

"Sure. But I'm older than you are and I can cope with it better."

"But, Uncle Douglas, I'm not artistic. I haven't any talent for anything."

Uncle Douglas patted me again. "Don't worry, duckling. That will come, too."

Uncle Douglas can always make me feel more than I am, as though I were really somebody. It's one of the very nicest things about him.

Rob came in just then and turned the volume up on the TV

again, so I kissed Uncle Douglas and went back out to the kitchen because I didn't feel like watching cartoons.

After a while Daddy came home and Mother told me to go up and tell Suzy and Maggy to wash their hands and get ready for dinner. I went into the bathroom with them to wash my hands, too. Suzy and Maggy were kind of giggling together while they washed up, as though they were sharing a secret they weren't going to let me in on, but after she'd dried her hands Maggy turned to me and her eyes seemed to grow very dark and big and she said, "My father's plane exploded yesterday."

"Yes," I said. I thought I ought to say something else, but I didn't know what else to say. You can't just politely say "I'm sorry," as though it were one of Rob's toy airplanes.

"If he hadn't died he was going to take me to the ocean for two weeks and I did want to go."

Now I could say, "I'm sorry."

"People ought to be sorry for me," Maggy said. "I'm an orphan."

"I'm sorry for you," Suzy said earnestly. "I'm terribly sorry for you, Maggy."

"So you'll be nice to me, won't you?" Maggy asked.

"Of course!"

I *was* sorry for her; with my mind I was sorry for her, but I wasn't feeling any empathy. And that was peculiar: here was Maggy, almost my age, only a couple of years younger, and her mother and father were both dead, and I couldn't think of anything more horrible in the world; and Aunt Elena was a grownup, so of course I couldn't feel about her the way I could about another girl. But it was Aunt Elena I ached over, and for Maggy I could feel only a strange bewilderment.

Mother called us down for dinner then, and after dinner Aunt Elena and Uncle Douglas left. The funeral was to be the next day, and Mother and Daddy were going down in the morning.

Bedtime was even stranger than it had been the night before. Mother read to us in Suzy's and my room, only now it wasn't Suzy's and my room, it was Suzy and Maggy's room. Suzy and Maggy giggled together while Mother read, and when I told them to be quiet so the rest of us could hear, Maggy said, "My, but she's bossy."

Suzy said, "I should think you'd be ashamed of yourself, Victoria Austin."

Rob said, "What for?"

And John said, "For crying out loud, all of you kids shut up."

Mother didn't say anything. She looked around at us with sort of a quizzical look on her face and went on reading.

Rob went to sleep right away; he always does. I was allowed to read till nine, but even after I turned out the light I couldn't sleep—partly, of course, because I'm older, but also, I wasn't used to being in John's bed. John has a big double bed, and Rob's, which is across the foot of it, is much, much smaller.

Rob has allergies and he often snores in the autumn, and he snored that night and it was a cold night again and he burrowed down under the covers and only a tuft of light brown hair showed and his snores sounded contented and comfortable. I could see him because we always have a night-light on in the bathroom all night, and it makes just enough light come into our bedrooms so you can see a little.

I was just about to settle myself and try to go to sleep when John tiptoed in. He had on blue jeans and his heavy red jacket, and he came over to the bed and whispered, "Get dressed in something warm—you know, jeans or slacks—and come on down," and disappeared.

I got up and dressed and went down the back stairs into the kitchen and Mother was standing there in her polo coat and she said, "Get your jacket, Vicky. I thought maybe you and John and I might take some blankets and just go sit outside and watch the sky."

"Can we go up Hawk," John asked, "and watch from the top of the ski trails?"

Mother hesitated. "Let me check with Daddy."

Daddy was in the study reading an article in a medical magazine, and he said to go on, he wasn't expecting any calls, but we'd better not stay more than half an hour; it was too cold, anyhow.

So we got in the station wagon, with Colette in my lap and Mr. Rochester in back sitting on the three army blankets we'd brought, and drove to Hawk. Hawk is a beautiful mountain with ski trails and picnic places, and from the fire lookout you can see five states, and we love to go there. When we got out of the car Colette dashed out and barked madly and rushed around in circles the way she always does, and Mr. Rochester bounded around, and Mother and John spread one of the blankets out on the grass and we sat down on it and put one of the other blankets about our shoulders and the other one over our laps. Mother sat in the middle and both of us sat as close to her as we possibly could. The sky would probably have been just as beautiful if we'd sat on the north lawn at home, but we could have seen the lights of the village, and up on the mountain it seemed as though we were miles and miles from everywhere. The sky was enormous and terribly high. It's a funny thing: the colder it gets, the farther away the sky seems and the farther off the stars look. The sky was so thick with them it was almost as though it had been snowing stars, and down below us there was a white fog, so it seemed as though we were looking out over a great lake. The Milky Way was a river of light, and John began pointing out the constellations, and I found the Big Dipper and the North Star and Cassiopeia's Chair and Scorpio and Sagittarius. Sagittarius is my favorite because it's my sign of the zodiac and I like the idea of aiming for the stars.

Mother said, "I know you're both very upset about Uncle Hal and Maggy's father. We all are. I thought maybe if we came and looked at the stars it would help us to talk about it a little."

Just then a shooting star flashed across the sky, and John said, "There's a shooting star and I don't know what to wish. I want to wish it back to before yesterday and that none of this would have happened, but I know it wouldn't work."

I said, "Mother, I don't understand it," and I began to shiver.

Mother said, "Sometimes it's very hard to see the hand of God instead of the blind finger of Chance. That's why I wanted to come out where we could see the stars."

"I talked to Aunt Elena for a while," John said, in a strained sort of voice, "when everybody else was busy. We took Mr. Rochester and Colette for a walk." Mr. Rochester came up to us then and lay down beside me with a thud, putting his heavy head across my knees. Colette was already cuddled up in Mother's lap. I looked toward John, and the lenses of his glasses glimmered in the starlight. "She said that she and Uncle Hal knew that they were living on borrowed time," John said. "They'd always hoped it would be longer than it was, but the way their lives were, they only lived together in snatches, anyhow. And she said she was grateful for every moment she'd ever had with him, and, even if it was all over, she wouldn't trade places with anybody in the world."

"She said that to you, John?" Mother asked.

"Yes," John said, and then another star shot across the sky, this time with a shower of sparks. We sat there, close, close, and it was as though we could feel the love we had for one another moving through our bodies, moving from me through Mother, from Mother to John, and back again. I could feel the love filling me, love for Mother and John, and for Daddy and Suzy and Rob, too. And I prayed, "Oh, God, keep us together, please keep us together, please keep us safe and well and together."

It was as though our thoughts were traveling to one another, too, because John said, "Oh, Mother, why do things have to change and be different!" He sounded quite violent. "I like us exactly the way we are, our family. Why do people have to die, and people grow up and get married, and everybody grow away from each other? I wish we could just go on being exactly the way we are!"

"But we can't," Mother said. "We can't stop on the road of Time. We have to keep on going. And growing up is all part of it, the exciting and wonderful business of being alive. We can't understand it, any of us, any more than we can understand why Uncle Hal and Maggy's father had to die. But being alive is a gift, the most wonderful and exciting gift in the world. And there'll undoubtedly be many other moments when you'll feel this same way, John, when you're grown up and have children of your own."

"I don't understand about anything," John said. "I don't understand about people dying, and I don't understand about families, about people being as close as we are, and then everybody growing up, and not having Rob a baby anymore, and having to go off and live completely different lives."

"But look how close Grandfather and I still are," Mother said.

John shook his head. "I know. But it isn't the same thing. It's not like when you were little."

"No," Mother said. "But if I'd never grown up and met Daddy and married him you wouldn't be here, or Vicky or Suzy or Rob, and we wouldn't be sitting up here on Hawk Mountain shivering and looking at the stars. And we must have been here at least half an hour. Time to go home."

We went home and then we just stood outside for a while. The moon was sailing high now, and the sky was clear above the black pines at the horizon, with Northern Lights, which we hadn't seen up on Hawk at all, sending occasional rays darting high up into the sky. Daddy had heard us drive up, and he came

36

out and stood with us, his arm about Mother. I'd never seen such a startlingly brilliant night, the fields and mountains washed in a flood of light. The shadows of trees and sunflowers were sharply black and stretched long and thin across the lawn. It was so beautiful that for the moment the beauty was all that mattered; it wasn't important that there were things we would never understand.

The Scream in the Office

I had thought, getting into bed after we came down from Hawk, that now everything was beginning to straighten out, that things would get back to the way they always were. But I guess it was just because I wanted to think it. And maybe it wasn't just Uncle Hal. Maybe it was because John was fifteen and I was twelve and everything was ready to change anyhow.

The first thing that happened was that I woke out of a deep sleep with my ears filled with ear-splitting screams. I sat up in bed, still so sleepy that I didn't know what was going on, only that something awful must be happening. The light switched on in Mother and Daddy's room, and then in the guest room, where John was, and I heard feet hurrying into the room where Suzy and Maggy were, and the screams went right on. I flung myself out of bed and ran in, too, my heart pounding, and Maggy was sitting up in bed screaming at the top of her lungs.

Daddy said, "John, Vicky, go back to your rooms." When

Daddy speaks that way, we hop. I heard him saying, "Margaret, you are to stop screaming by the time I count to three." He counted slowly, "One, two, three," and Maggy was quiet as suddenly as though Daddy had turned off a faucet, and then she bellowed, "My mother's dead and my father's dead and you should be sorry for me!"

Daddy's voice was very quiet, but I could hear every word. "Maggy, no matter what bad things happen to us—and very bad things have happened to you—we still have to have a certain amount of consideration for other people. There are six people in this house besides you who are trying to sleep and who need their sleep. Suppose you come downstairs with me for a few minutes and we will see if we can't get you calmed down. Meanwhile, Suzy, I want you to go back to sleep. Maggy is not going to make any more disturbances tonight."

Daddy kept Maggy downstairs for quite a while; I was half asleep when I heard them coming back up. There wasn't a sound out of Maggy as Daddy tucked her in, and after the light went out in Mother and Daddy's bedroom a moment later, there wasn't another sound that night.

In the morning Mother had on a dark dress instead of a skirt and sweater, and she and Daddy drove us to school instead of letting us walk down the half mile to the school bus as usual. This was so they could introduce Maggy to Suzy's teacher. They'd had a talk with the principal the evening before and decided that Maggy would start in Suzy's grade; it would make it easier for her to be in with someone she knew. Mother and Daddy said they'd be back in time for dinner and that I was to start the potatoes, and John and I were to take care of the little ones. Rob was at a neighbor's until I got home from school; I was to pick him up on my way. I felt distinctly nervous about an afternoon with Maggy without Mother and Daddy, and I had a feeling that John did, too.

After school, Maggy and Suzy and I got off the school bus and started up the hill to our house. John goes to the Regional High School and he doesn't get home till after four, so I had over an hour to be in charge and I didn't like the idea a bit. Suzy will do what John says, but she almost always argues with me or just doesn't pay attention. And with Maggy to boss her around, heaven knew what she'd do. I felt distinctly trepidatious.

We stopped for Rob. He had Elephant's Child with him. As usual. Elephant's Child is an elephant that used to be blue but is now gray—a more ordinary color for elephants, anyhow—and it has a music box inside that plays Brahms's *Lullaby*, and Rob adores it. He's had it since he was a baby, and he's always been very careful of it and never over-wound it, and it still played all of its tune—something that Suzy's and my music-box toys never did, because we always managed to break them.

As soon as Maggy saw Elephant's Child she wanted to hold it. Now, maybe it wasn't very generous of Rob to say no, and pull away, and hold Elephant's Child even closer to him, but in his place I think I'd have felt exactly the same way.

Maggy pouted, but she didn't say anything and kept on walking up the hill, just behind Rob. When we were almost at the house she reached out and grabbed Elephant's Child and raced on ahead with it, laughing in a horrid, screechy way, keeping just out of reach of Rob and winding the key to make Elephant's Child play.

Suzy didn't say anything, but she looked troubled. Rob howled. I was no good at all, because both Rob and Maggy were making so much noise no one could hear me. Finally I made myself heard over the din. "Give it to him, Maggy, please!" Maggy flung Elephant's Child in the vague general direction of Rob, and it landed in the middle of a barberry bush. Rob plunged in after it, getting all scratched up and howling louder. I finally managed to get everybody herded into the house. I may get mad at John at times, but I'd have given anything in the world to have had him walk in at that moment. Rob was sobbing, "He's broken! Elephant's Child is broken!"

"Give him to me, Rob, let me see," I said.

He handed me Elephant's Child, and I twisted the music-box key and it just went around and around the way those things do when they've been too roughly handled, and Brahms's *Lullaby* didn't play.

"Oh, Rob," I said helplessly. "Maybe Mother or Daddy can fix him."

"Let *me* see," Suzy said. "I bet he isn't broken at all. We're just making a fuss over nothing and making Maggy feel bad. I bet I can make him work."

"Okay, Doc," I said. "You try."

"Well . . ." Suzy said, when she realized the music-box part of Elephant's Child was indeed broken.

Rob had stopped yelling. He took Elephant's Child from Suzy and held him close and went into the study and sat down in the big black leather chair and put his head down against Elephant's Child, and I could see that his lip was quivering and tears were sliding down his cheeks, but he wasn't making any sound.

And I wasn't feeling any empathy about Maggy at all.

"What a lot of fuss about a stupid old toy," Maggy said crossly. "Can't your mother and father get him another?"

"I suppose if you break a toy you just get another one?" I demanded angrily.

"Of course."

There was no use saying that we didn't, and that even if Mother and Daddy could get Rob another Elephant's Child it wouldn't be the same.

"Maggy didn't mean to break it," Suzy said, but her voice was uncertain. "Don't make her feel bad."

As far as I could see, Maggy didn't feel bad at all. "Do you two have any homework?" I asked them.

"Just some spelling words."

"Well, get them done, then."

"Let's play first," Maggy said. "We can play hospital again. Come on, Suzy."

"We're supposed to do our homework before we play," I said.

But Maggy had already started upstairs, and Suzy went after her.

"Suzy," I shouted, "Mother'll be furious if you don't get your homework done."

"I'll do it later, silly," Suzy called back, and ran after Maggy.

I went in to Rob. He was still crying silently, and when I tried to comfort him he pushed me away. I brought in my homework and sat down at the desk near him, but I couldn't concentrate on anything properly. After a while he got up and climbed into my lap and put his arms around my neck and I felt better.

I thought I ought to go upstairs and check on Suzy and Maggy, but I could hear them playing, and I decided that as long as there weren't any horrible screams I'd just leave them alone. Rob got out his wooden trains and set them up on the floor by me, and I worked on my homework till John got home.

I could hear him hanging up his things, and then he came into the study and dumped his books down. "How're you making out, Vicky? Everything sounds okay. Hi, Robbie, old man."

I looked at him glumly. "As a baby sitter I'm a complete flop."

"Why?"

I told him what had happened. "And I wasn't any help at all," I finished. "I was worse than no good. Thank heavens you're home, John. I don't know what I'd have done if she started anything else."

John was examining Elephant's Child. "One thing's for sure," he said, putting Elephant's Child down. "She's a spoiled brat from way back."

"What's the matter with her, anyhow?" I asked John. "Do you suppose this is just the way she is—I mean, spoiled rotten and everything—or do you suppose it's because of her mother and father?"

"Well," John said slowly, "how would we feel if . . ."

"Stop," I said quickly. "Stop."

"She does make it rough," John said. "I know I'm not as sorry for her as I ought to be."

43

"Yeah, that worries me," I said. "Suzy feels all sorry for her the way I ought to, and I can't seem to make myself."

"I suppose the thing to do," John said, "is to try to think how we'd feel if it was one of us. I mean, if there weren't four of us, if none of the rest of you had been born, I might be spoiled rotten, too."

"That's a nasty thought," I said. "Not so much you being spoiled as the rest of us not being born."

"Sometimes I'd be just as happy if you hadn't been," John said, and I was about to make an angry retort when he said, "Oh, let's not fight, Vic. You know I didn't mean it. I'd better go upstairs and check on those two now."

When he came down he said, "Well, they're happily tearing up Suzy's best doll so Suzy can do an operation." Usually Suzy operates on dolls that get broken somehow or other. I didn't think just deliberately destroying one was such a hot idea, and I didn't think Suzy would, either, when it was all done and too late. But John and I thought, under the circumstances, we'd just let it go.

"I know what you mean," I said grimly. "Let's keep peace and quiet at all costs. I think I'd better go fix the potatoes now before anything else happens. I'd hate to have Mother and Daddy get back and find I hadn't done *anything* they asked me to."

"I'll help you," John said unexpectedly. His jobs are things like chopping wood and keeping the wood basket filled and mowing lawns and shoveling snow. We got out the scrapers and set to.

"Sounds funny without Mother playing records," John said. "Shall I put something on?"

"Uh-huh."

John put on *Rosenkavalier,* and I was glad, because it's lovely and gay, and I wasn't in the mood for anything that wasn't, and the sound of it made the house feel better, somehow.

Well, we had only one more crisis, and that was when John tried to get Maggy and Suzy to do their homework before they watched *Mickey Mouse Club.* But he gave up, and we sat in the kitchen and realized we were starved because we'd forgotten to have anything to eat when we got home from school. So we had milk and cookies and took some in to Rob and Suzy and Maggy, and Maggy and Rob fought over them and we wished we hadn't. I don't know when we've been as glad to see Mother and Daddy as we were when they walked in at six.

After Mother had read to us and the three little ones were in bed, John and I went back downstairs in our nightclothes. Mother said that as long as I was sleeping in with Rob I could stay up half an hour later, and John stays up till he gets his homework done. If I think I have a lot now, what'll I do when I get to high school? Daddy said that since Suzy and Maggy had not done their homework they would simply have to tell their teacher that they had played instead, and take the consequences. Neither of them liked that one bit. They wanted to sit up late and do it, but Daddy said no.

"How about you kids," Daddy asked John and me. "You about through?"

"I didn't have very much today," I said. "I'm all done."

"John?"

"I just have to finish a book report."

"Let's talk for a few minutes, then." He put another log on the fire and sat down. Mother turned from getting things ready for breakfast and sat down, too.

"So you had a rough time this afternoon, didn't you?" Daddy asked us. We nodded. He thought for a minute, then he said, "The way things stand now, it looks as though Maggy will be with us for quite a while, and it's going to be an adjustment for all of us. But we must remember that it's going to be an adjustment for Maggy most of all. Now, I know you're both very sorry for her—"

John broke in, "But that's the trouble, Dad. We aren't. We try to be, but we aren't."

"And at school today, Daddy," I said, "at recess, she kept sort of bragging about it, and telling people—about her parents being dead, I mean, and her father's plane having exploded."

"She was a new girl in a new school," Daddy said. "Maybe that was all she had to brag about."

"I don't think Vic or I would," John said. "If anything happened to you or Mother I don't think we'd go around talking about it to people."

"Now, wait a minute, John," Daddy said. "I was just about Maggy's age when my mother died when Uncle Douglas was born. And it was inconceivable to me that everybody in the world didn't know about it, that anybody could be unaware that my mother was dead. And when the paper boy came by our house that night, he didn't know, and he called out to me just as usual, as though nothing at all had happened, and I was embarrassed for him, that he shouldn't know about an event that must surely rock the foundations of the universe. And I told him that my mother was dead, and I'm sure I felt more a sense of importance than grief."

"Grief for the big things takes a long time to come," Mother said. "You know how, when you cut yourself badly, you don't feel it at all for a long time? It doesn't hurt till the numbness wears off? Grief is like that."

"Yeah, I think I see," John said slowly.

"On the other hand," Mother went on, "I don't think Maggy's reactions to her tragedy are quite the same as yours were, Wallace, or as our children's would be. For one thing, she'd only been with her father for a month when the accident happened. She'd never known him at all before then."

"Never known her father! But——" I started.

"Okay, Vicky," Daddy said, "let's let Mother tell you a little something about Maggy's background. I think it will help you to understand why she is the way she is. We must all try very hard to understand, because we can't have any one child, no matter how tragic her circumstances, disrupting an entire family."

"She's made a good start," John said.

"Suppose you'd never known what it was like to be loved?" Mother asked him. "Suppose you never saw Daddy, and I spent all my time going to parties and on cruises and left you with nurses and governesses and did my best to forget I had any children?"

"I'm glad you don't," John said.

"But that's what it was like for Maggy," Mother told us. "All the toys and clothes in the world and not one moment of

47

spontaneous family love. None of the easy security you children take for granted. She had dinner with her grandfather every Sunday. That was as close to family life as she got."

"Did her grandfather love her?" I asked.

"In his way, I think he did, very much. But he's evidently not a bit like our darling Grandfather, Vic, if that's what you're thinking. He's solitary and strict and stern. And he'd had a bad heart attack just at the time of Maggy's mother's death, which was why she went to her father at that time."

"How . . . how did her mother die?" John asked.

"Of pneumonia, while she was traveling in Spain."

"All this help you to understand a little?" Daddy asked.

"Yes," I said.

"But how come she's living with us?" John asked. "And for how long?"

"Her grandfather is still ill," Daddy said, "so we'll just have to take things as they come, from day to day. Dick Hamilton was overjoyed when his little girl came to live with him, just a month before he died. And he had no idea how to handle her at all, except to give in to her completely, to give her whatever she wanted the minute she wanted it. At least he gave her love, real love, which was something she'd never had before, and Elena feels sure that, given time, things would have worked out, that he'd realize he was spoiling her just as she'd always been spoiled. But he wasn't given time."

Daddy paused and John said, "Doesn't her grandfather want her as soon as he's well? I mean, wouldn't that be the logical thing? If he has lots of money and everything, she wouldn't be in his way."

"No, she wouldn't, and it would be a pretty sad life for a child, wouldn't it? Maybe Mr. Ten Eyck—that's his name—realizes this. We aren't sure yet."

"What do you mean?"

"You see," Daddy said, "Dick Hamilton didn't have any family at all, nobody who belonged to him who could take care of Maggy if anything should happen to him. And in the nature of his work he knew that something might happen to him at any time. So he asked Aunt Elena and Uncle Hal if they would be responsible for her. In his will he has asked that they be her legal guardians."

"Then why doesn't Aunt Elena take her, if that's what he wanted?" John asked.

"It isn't as easy as that, John," Daddy said. "In the first place, legally, a wish like that isn't binding. You can will your property, but, according to the law, you cannot will a person. You can only express a wish. In the second place, Aunt Elena doesn't have Uncle Hal anymore. She's all alone. She leaves for a nationwide concert tour next month, and she has a living to earn. And for her own sake she needs her music right now."

"So it's all a mess, isn't it?" John asked.

"Yes. And Aunt Elena's doing what she can to make it a little less of a mess. She has paid us the great compliment of thinking that this is the place where Maggy can best learn to live the normal life she's never known."

"Or we can learn to be abnormal," John muttered.

Daddy laughed and said, "I hope you have stronger personalities than that. Mother and Aunt Elena and Uncle Douglas and I had a talk with Mr. Ten Eyck this afternoon. Legally he's her next of kin, and the decision has to come from him. Whether Maggy'll be with us for a couple of weeks, or months, or a year, we don't know. This is just a temporary solution until he's well enough to decide what he thinks is best."

"That's quite a story," John said. "What do *you* think is best, Dad?"

"I don't know, John," Daddy said slowly. "As I said, the only thing to do right now is to take things simply, from day to day."

"Well, I do feel sorry for her now," John said. "I guess that will help."

Well, sure it helped, but it seemed to John and me it needed a lot more than that, or maybe we didn't have the strong personalities Daddy thought we did. Oh, it wasn't all as wild as it was right there in the beginning; things kind of got into a groove; and, as Mother and Daddy said, it certainly was a challenge; but it seemed that no matter where you turned in the house, Maggy was always there. There seemed to be more of Maggy than the rest of us put together. If Mother wanted to play the piano or her guitar, Maggy wanted to play them, too. When Daddy came home at dinnertime and swung Rob, Maggy had to be swung, too, though even Suzy knows she's much too big and heavy for that sort of thing. One thing John made very clear right from the start was that Maggy was not to go out to the barn and touch his space suit, and I think he scared her into realizing that that was one thing she'd better not do. I didn't blame John for being ferocious with her about it, because Maggy couldn't seem to keep her hands off things, just picking them up and touching them, things off Mother's dressing table, Rob's toys, my books.

One rainy November afternoon after school I was doing homework, John wasn't home yet, and Rob was sitting on the kitchen stool playing records on his little player. Mother was making Spanish rice and Rob kept asking her what he should play for her next, and none of us thought much about Suzy and Maggy. We thought they were up in their room playing dolls or hospital. I have to admit they played awfully well together, much better than Suzy and I ever did. Maggy would decide what kind of game she wanted to play, but Suzy could always be the doctor, and as long as she was boss in that part of the game it was okay for Maggy to be boss in the rest of it. Of course, Suzy got to the point where she wouldn't let Maggy break any more of her toys, but a great enormous box of Maggy's own toys came up from New York and Maggy didn't mind breaking them a bit. She said she could always just write and ask her grandfather for more. Naturally, Mother and Daddy tried to discourage this, but some doll or other always seemed to be battered up "by accident."

When John got home that afternoon he made himself a bacon, lettuce, and tomato sandwich, and then said he was going up to his room to do his homework.

"Just look in Suzy and Maggy's room and check on what they're doing," Mother said. "They're being unnaturally quiet."

After a moment or two John called down that they weren't in their room.

"Well, where are they, then?" Mother demanded. "See if you can round them up for me, Vicky."

I went upstairs and looked all around but they weren't anywhere. They weren't anywhere downstairs, either. I thought they must be playing a game and hiding on us just to scare us, so I looked under all the beds and in all the closets, but I couldn't find them.

"If they've gone out in all this rain I'll beat them to a pulp and spread them on my toast like strawberry jam," Mother said crossly. "Stir this for me, Vicky, and see that it doesn't burn. I'd better go out and look."

"I'll go," I said.

"No, honey, you just stir for me."

Mother put on a raincoat and a scarf around her head, took the dogs, and went out. From the windows I could see her walking about outside in the drenching downpour and calling. She came back in and stood by the closet, stamping and shaking off rain, so that before she had hung up her things she was standing in a little puddle of water that had dripped from her. "Get a towel and dry Colette," she said, as she gave Rochester a rub until he was dry enough to come in before the kitchen fire to dry the rest of the way.

John came down, saying, "Those girls still missing?"

"Yes," Mother said, and I could see that she was worried.

"I'll look," John said. "Did you go into the barn, Mother?"

"No."

"If they've gone in there and are at my space suit—" John started, and shoved into his jacket.

But they weren't in the barn. "I've got an idea," John said, and went into Daddy's office.

Daddy's main office is down in Clovenford, which is a much bigger place than Thornhill, and where the hospital is; but he has a small office here at the house.

John went through the waiting room and into the office, and Maggy and Suzy were there, playing. They had Maggy's biggest doll down on Daddy's examining table, and they were in the middle of an operation, and Suzy was using Daddy's instruments from the sterilizer.

I don't think I've ever, ever, seen Mother so angry. We're *never* allowed to play in Daddy's office, or even to go in it without permission. Suzy knows that. Maggy knew it, too, because I'd heard Daddy telling her so. Well, it was obvious they both knew it, because they'd put on their raincoats and gone in from the outside entrance so nobody would see them, and their things lay in wet puddles on the floor.

Mother said, "I'm too angry to spank you, or even to think of spanking you. Your father will do that when he gets home. Go upstairs, both of you, and get into your pajamas. Maggy, get into your own bed and stay there until I tell you to get out of it. Suzy, you will please come back downstairs and you may lie on the couch in the waiting room with a blanket. I don't want you to be near each other, and I want you to think, both of you, think seriously."

They started to pick up their wet things.

"No," Mother said. "Leave everything where it is. I want your father to see everything just as you've left it. Go in through the house and do as I say. At once."

They did. At once. I've never seen Maggy hop so fast.

When they were in bed Maggy began to howl—loud dramatic sobs. In the office waiting room Suzy lay on the couch with her face to the wall and didn't move or make a sound. Mother completely ignored Maggy's howls. John brought his books down to the study.

"I'm sorry, John," Mother said. "You'll just have to concentrate as best you can."

"It's okay, Mother," John said rather grimly. "As long as it isn't driving you crazy, it doesn't bother me one bit."

After she'd howled for about half an hour Maggy came down the back stairs, pouting prettily to Mother. "I'm awfully sorry, Aunt Victoria. We didn't know we were being bad."

"Get back upstairs and into bed," Mother said.

"But I said I was sorry, Aunt Victoria!"

"I'm glad you're sorry, Maggy, but get back upstairs and into bed, anyhow. I will tell you when I think it's time for you to come down."

Mother spoke very quietly, very coldly, and Maggy obeyed. Up in bed she started to yowl again, but this time it didn't last as long.

Rob had stopped playing records and suddenly we noticed that his lip was trembling.

"Rob, darling, what is it?" Mother asked.

"I want to go in to Suzy," Rob said.

"I'm sorry, Rob, but you must leave Suzy alone."

Rob got down from his stool, ran to Mother, flung his arms around her legs, and butted his head against her. "But I want to go to Suzy!"

Mother untangled him. "No, Rob. Suzy has to stay by herself. Come on, let's go to the piano, Rob, and we'll play some songs till Daddy gets back. Want to come, Vic?"

I knew we were singing the songs for Suzy and Maggy as well as to amuse Rob and keep him from being upset. Daddy was home earlier than usual that evening, but it seemed as though it was ever so much later. John came in and sang with us, *Cockles and Mussels*, and *The Eddystone Light*, and *You Take the High Road*, all the old favorites, and when Daddy came in he said, "Well, this is a nice family picture! Where're the two little girls?"

So Mother told him.

I was awfully glad I wasn't Suzy or Maggy. It wasn't so much the spanking. It was the talking-to.

"Those were not toys you were playing with," I heard Daddy say as he went into the office with them. "People's lives depend on those instruments. When I made a rule that you were not to play in the office, I made it for that reason. You knew this, Suzy, and it was up to you to explain it to Maggy."

Then the door shut firmly behind them.

But that wasn't quite the end, either of the spankings or of the screaming.

For the first time that evening we could tell that Maggy felt bad about something. Suzy wasn't the only subdued one with red-rimmed eyes at dinner. For once, instead of trying to monopolize the conversation, Maggy just sat there and ate.

And then what she did next was something none of the rest of us could or would have done. Only Maggy would do something like that.

Daddy had office hours at home that night; he does twice a week. He started right after dinner. The office lights shine onto the catalpa tree outside Rob and John's—only now it was Rob's and my—room. I lay in bed and listened to Rob snore and looked at the light from the office as it splashed yellow on the big leaves of the catalpa tree. I felt cozy and sleepy, and I was getting used to being in John's big bed instead of my own. The big bed and Rob's little one are a soft, goldeny pine, and two of the walls are pine, too, satin-smooth old boards almost two feet wide. The other two walls are papered with blue paper with a white snowflake pattern. On the wall opposite the bed there's a big picture of a sailing ship with full white sails and blue water and skies and white clouds scudding.

Anyhow, I lay there in the big bed when suddenly there was a scream, a piercing scream, not a Maggy scream, but a scream that wasn't like anything I'd ever heard before. I sat up, wide awake, and the scream came again. It came from the direction of Daddy's office and I didn't know what could have happened. Nobody'd ever screamed that way before, even little kids with shots. I heard feet running and I knew Mother was dashing to see what was the matter. And John went thudding downstairs. Rob didn't move and for a moment I was too scared to. Then I got out of bed and hurried downstairs after John and almost bumped into Mother and she said, very sharply, "Vicky, get back into bed. At once."

"But what's happened? What is it?"

"I'll tell you later," she said. "Get upstairs to bed." It was the quiet voice, so I turned around to go back up, and just then

Daddy came through the living room, pushing Maggy in front of him.

"John, Vicky, get upstairs at once," Daddy said, and we turned and ran. John came in and sat on his bed with me. We'd peeped into Suzy's room and she was asleep. Once Suzy goes to sleep she's like Rob; nothing wakes her.

John said, "Hold it while I get my glasses. I was so scared I forgot them."

I knew then he'd been good and scared. John is so nearsighted he can't see two feet without them, and putting them on as he gets out of bed is a reflex. I could hear him bumping into something and then he came back in, pushing his glasses up his nose with one hand and rubbing his shin with the other. "What on earth——" he started, and then we heard Maggy yelling. It was a good solid yell this time, nothing imaginary or hysterical about it.

"I bet Daddy's giving her Hades," John said.

"But why . . . what do you suppose she did——"

Mother came up then and looked in and said automatically, "Whisper so you won't wake Rob," and sat by John on the foot of the bed.

"What happened?" we both asked.

In the light from the bathroom and the light from Daddy's office windows I couldn't tell whether Mother was trying not to smile or not. She said, "Daddy's speaking to Maggy."

"What'd she do?"

"She said she wanted to be near Daddy to show him she was sorry, so she sneaked into the waiting room and crawled

57

under the couch, and Mrs. Elliott was sitting on it waiting to see Daddy, and Maggy bit her on the ankle. Twice."

John and I both giggled. We couldn't help it. Mrs. Elliott weighs over two hundred pounds. She teaches singing at school and she's always going on about how she loves little children and none of us likes her. As a matter of fact, we can't stand her.

"Did she draw blood?" John asked.

"*Really,* John!" Mother exclaimed. "Maggy has frightened Mrs. Elliott into hysterics. You mustn't laugh, it's very rude. I've got to go back downstairs now and help Daddy cope with Mrs. Elliott, but I knew you two wouldn't go to sleep until you knew what had happened. John, go get back into bed. Vicky, lie down and go to sleep. I might as well take Rob to the bathroom now."

She sat Rob up in bed and in his sleep he put his arms around her and gave her a big kiss; he can be very sweet as well as perfectly awful. Then she stood him up and walked him, still in his sleep, to the bathroom, and the minute he got back into bed he started snoring loudly. "I'd better get Daddy to give him an antihistamine tomorrow night," Mother said absently, and bent down and kissed Rob. Then she kissed me, and as she left I could hear Daddy bringing Maggy up to bed.

"I meant to hurt her," I heard Maggy saying.

"I know," Daddy said. "But no matter what Mrs. Elliott said, there was no excuse for your behavior, Maggy. She's going to have a bad bruise where you bit her."

"She said my father's plane couldn't have gone to another star. I was telling the kids about it at recess, and she was listening and said it couldn't be true and I hate her." Now Maggy started to cry, really to cry, in a different way than we'd ever heard her cry, not shrieking and yelling, but crying as though it came all the way up from her stomach, and Daddy didn't say anything, and I knew he was just sitting there with his arms around her. After a while the crying stopped and I heard her saying to Daddy, "I love you," and Daddy said, "I love you, too, Maggy." And then there was silence, and after a while I heard Daddy get up and leave the room. John came out to meet him at the head of the stairs.

"Dad, it was my fault," John said.

"What was your fault, John?"

"About the stars. You know what I told you last year—how I'd figured out that after we died we maybe went to different stars to kind of go on learning?"

"You told Maggy this?"

"She asked me," John said. "She wanted to know, if her father's plane had exploded in the middle of the sky, what had happened to him and where he had gone, and I said maybe he'd gone to live on another star. And I guess she thought the plane had gone on to another star. I'm sorry, Dad, I didn't mean—"

"That's all right, John," Daddy said. "We'll talk more about it tomorrow. It was good for Maggy to cry it out the way she did just now. I've got to get back down to Mrs. Elliott."

"Mother's with her."

"Yes, I know. Good night, John."

John came back in to me and sat on the foot of the bed again. "That blasted Elliott," he muttered. "She never could

59

keep her mouth shut. No matter what she thinks, she didn't have any right to upset Maggy about her father. I don't blame her for biting." Then he began to giggle again, and I began to giggle, too, and we were both holding each other and rocking back and forth in a fit of laughter.

The Terrible Week

There's a family story about me when I was Rob's age or younger. I'd done something I shouldn't have done, and I'd been spanked, and I climbed up into Daddy's lap that evening and twined my arms around his neck and said, "Daddy, why is it I'm so much nicer *after* I've been spanked?"

Well, Maggy was ever so much nicer for a long time after that. She stopped grumbling over making her own bed, and she did her share of setting the table, and she didn't break nearly as many things.

Then we had a terrible week. It all began with Suzy. We were reading E. B. White's *Charlotte's Web* aloud, and one evening early in January we came to the part about Charlotte's death. And Suzy cried. She didn't cry when Uncle Hal died, but she cried, hard, about the spider. And this is not like Suzy. She never cries over books. But she always seems to care more about animals than she does about people, anyhow. She's the one who feeds the cats every night, and she's the reason we have so many cats, because each time Mother and Daddy threaten to get rid of any of them she carries on so. She wouldn't even let them get rid of Prunewhip, and everybody had to admit Prunewhip's about the ugliest cat anybody's ever seen.

So she carried on over Charlotte.

Mother tried to explain to her that according to the spider calendar Charlotte had lived to be a very old lady and had had a fine life and lived to be as old as any spider does and older than many. But that only partly comforted her.

Then we came to the problem of Charlotte's friend, Wilbur, the pig.

All teary, Suzy asked, "Mother, why did Mr. Zuckerman want to kill Wilbur?"

"Well, Mr. Zuckerman was a farmer, and farmers do kill pigs and sell them for meat."

"Have we ever eaten pig?"

"Yes. Often."

"When?"

"Well, whenever we have ham, that's pig. Or bacon. Or pork chops. Or sausage."

"I *hate* sausage."

Sausage is one of Suzy's favorite things.

But after everybody had gone to bed and Rob was asleep, John came back in. "Vicky?"

"Hello."

"Not asleep?"

"Nope."

John climbed onto the foot of the bed and pulled the quilt over him. "I know how Suzy feels about sausage," he said.

I'd been almost asleep, so it took me a minute to tumble to what he meant. Then I said, "Me, too. But it doesn't stop me from eating it. Or steak, even though I get terribly fond of the cows we see in the north field every summer."

"You know," John said, "there are lots of people in the world who are vegetarians. They don't eat meat or anything but vegetables at all. And there are people who eat chicken and fish but no red meat. And there are people who can't eat pig. Suzy would like that. But I don't think that's any answer. You can't just not eat some things and eat other things."

"Like what?" I said.

"Well, like anything. Even lettuce or spinach. They're alive. They're just as alive in their own way as a cow is in its way. Or a pig like Wilbur."

"Then you'd starve to death," I said.

"Yeah. So we eat steak."

"And turkey. And tomatoes. And they all taste wonderful."

"Grandfather talks about a choice of evils," John said. "Maybe that's it. We have to choose between eating something that's alive or starving to death. But I love eating, Vic. It doesn't seem an evil to me. I don't mean I just love the food, but the family part of it. The sitting around the table and talking and being together."

"Next time we go to Grandfather's you'd better ask him," I said. "But remember in the Bible there's a lot about Jesus' eating? Getting together with His friends and disciples and sitting down to eat and teach. Grandfather talked about that once. And you remember—is it Arabs? I think it's Arabs—anyhow, if someone's eaten bread with them, broken bread, they can't do him any harm."

But now John was getting sleepy. "That was awfully good shepherd's pie we had for dinner," he murmured.

I kicked him through the covers. "Get back to your own room before you fall asleep."

So we kept right on eating and liking it, too. But Suzy wouldn't eat any bacon the next morning, or sausage, or anything to do with pig all that week. And she seemed sort of cranky and not like herself. And one night when it was bedtime she said she had a stomachache.

Then, one evening after we'd all sat down to dinner, Mother said, "I found a whole pile of bubble gum and candy in one of the boots in the pantry. I was trying to create a little order out of chaos, and I hardly think a boot that is supposed to keep your feet warm and dry is a place for things like that. Whose is it?"

Her voice was perfectly pleasant, but it was a little too quiet for comfort. Nobody said anything.

Daddy said, "It sounds rather like hoarding to me, anyhow. How about it? Who's the culprit?"

Still nobody said anything.

Mother said, "I didn't realize I was starting anything. You're allowed to buy candy with your allowance. I just want to know who's been putting it in a boot."

I wasn't the one, so I looked curiously and a little anxiously around the table at everybody else. I saw that John was looking

64

around, too. Suzy was staring straight ahead with a set expression, and Maggy was staring at Suzy.

Rob said, "I didn't do it." He couldn't very well. His allowance is six cents, five cents for Sunday school and a penny for emptying the wastepaper baskets every Saturday morning. Maggy gets five dollars from Mr. Ten Eyck every week, but Mother and Daddy put four dollars and seventy-five cents of it in the bank for her, so she only has a quarter to spend, like Suzy.

We all knew it was Suzy, but Daddy said, "John, do you know anything about this?"

"No, Daddy."

"Vicky?"

"No, Daddy."

"Maggy?"

Maggy looked down at her plate, across at Suzy, and down at her plate again. She didn't say anything.

"Did you put the candy and gum in the boot?" Daddy asked.

"No, Uncle Wallace."

"Suzy?"

"No," Suzy said, and didn't look at him.

"No what, Suzy?"

"I don't know anything about it," Suzy said.

"About what?"

"About who took the candy and put it in the boot."

"*Took* the candy?"

Suzy didn't answer.

"Whose boot was it?" Daddy asked Mother.

"Rob's."

Rob has more than once been known to confuse the truth with his imagination, but he was looking right at Daddy now, and anyhow we all knew it was Suzy, and that it was more than buying candy and gum with her allowance and saving it in the boot.

Mother said, "Suzy, why don't you tell us about it?"

Suzy shouted out, "I haven't anything to tell!" and got up so roughly that she knocked her chair over, and ran pounding upstairs, where we could hear her crying at the top of her lungs.

Maggy said, "Suzy took the candy from the store."

Daddy said, "Don't tell us about it, please, Maggy. We want Suzy to tell us."

"But she stole it," Maggy started.

"Margaret. I said that we want Suzy to tell us."

Upstairs, Suzy was still crying at the top of her lungs. Mother started to push back her chair to go up to her, but Daddy said, "Leave her alone, Vic. We haven't finished eating dinner yet."

It had started out to be such a nice family meal. And now we were all upset. Rob got up and started for the stairs, and Daddy shouted, "Robert, sit down!"

And Rob said, "But I want to go to Suzy."

"Leave Suzy alone," Daddy said, "and finish your dinner."

We had strawberry mousse for dessert, and none of us enjoyed it. Suzy kept crying, and Mother finished her dessert and said, "Excuse me, Wally. You children do the dishes tonight, please," and went upstairs.

We did the dishes with a lot better grace than usual. Daddy went into the study to read and Rob played records. He'd played *Pinocchio* three times from beginning to end before Mother and Suzy came back downstairs.

"Where's Daddy?" Mother asked.

"In the study."

"Well, let's all go in, then," Mother said. "Suzy has something to say."

We went in and Mother took Suzy firmly by the hand and they followed us.

"Suzy has something to tell us all," Mother said.

Suzy stood there, gulping, and finally she flung herself into Daddy's lap and just sobbed over and over, "I'm sorry, Daddy, I'm sorry, I'm sorry, I'm sorry."

Daddy held her for a moment, and then he put her on the floor in front of him, between his knees, saying, "I know you're sorry, Suzy, and I'm glad, but I think you'd better tell me what you're sorry about." Suzy kept on crying and hiccuping, and Daddy said firmly, "Suzy, don't you think you'd better stop this and get it over with?"

So Suzy said, "I went into the store after Brownies, and I went into the store after choir, and I took candy and gum and put them in my pocket, and then when I got home I hid them in Rob's boot because those boots are too small and he hardly ever wears them anymore."

"You mean you bought them with your allowance?" Daddy asked.

"No," Suzy said. "I took them. And I'm going to Mr. and Mrs. Jenkins at the store and I'm going to tell them what I did and pay for them, all the ones I still have, and all the ones I ate, and I'll never do it again." And she started to cry again.

"Suzy," Daddy said, "you are to stop crying or you'll make yourself sick."

"I can't," Suzy said.

"But you must." He waited until Suzy had stopped, and then he said, "You know you did two things that were wrong, don't you? First in taking—stealing—from Mrs. Jenkins, and second, in not telling the truth when Mother asked you about it."

"I know," Suzy whispered.

Daddy looked at her for a long moment. Then he said, "All right, Suzy. You say that you'll never do it again, and I believe you. And I want you to promise that you'll always tell the truth to Mother and me, too. No matter what you've done, you only make it worse if you try to lie your way out."

"I never lie," Maggy said righteously.

Daddy looked at her sharply. "Never?" he asked. "Think that one over, Margaret."

"Are you going to punish me?" Suzy asked.

"Mother has asked you to go to Mr. and Mrs. Jenkins, and you're going. That's all. I think you've punished yourself enough. But why, Suzy? Why did you take it? Can you tell me? Do you know?"

That was something we all wondered. We couldn't blame this one on Maggy; she didn't have anything to do with it. But I couldn't help wondering if she hadn't put the idea into Suzy's head. But maybe that's not fair. Suzy could have got the idea from other people, too. Nanny Jenkins told me that sometimes her mother and father do have trouble with children taking candy and things. Nanny says if her father didn't have his cello, running the store would drive him crazy.

Suzy shook her head. "I was hungry," she said.

So maybe that was it, because she hadn't been eating nearly as much on account of Wilbur the pig.

"What happened to your allowance?" Daddy asked.

"After Sunday school and Brownies there's only fifteen cents," Suzy said.

"That's plenty for candy," Daddy told her. "No wonder you've been cross and unlike yourself all week and had a stomachache the other night."

"It wasn't just my stomach," Suzy said. "I think it was a heartache, too."

Finally Daddy smiled. "Now go to bed, Suzy, and go right to sleep. It's time for all you little ones to be in bed. Past time, and tomorrow's a school day."

But that was only the beginning.

The next night at dinner everything was fine until Suzy started on about her twentieth carrot stick. She was hungry because she still wasn't eating pig because of Wilbur, and we had a pork roast and applesauce that night, so she really attacked that carrot stick.

John said, "You won't eat pig because of Wilbur but you don't mind chomping down on that poor piece of carrot. And it doesn't bother you to think of a potato being roasted."

Suzy got kind of pink and then white. "It's not the same thing," she said.

"Why isn't it?" John asked. "Vicky and I were talking about it the other night. Carrots and potatoes grow. They're alive. If you're going to stop eating pig because of Wilbur you ought to stop eating carrots, too. And applesauce. We got to know those apples very well last summer when they were on our trees, but that didn't stop us from taking a knife and tearing off their skins and slashing them up."

"John!" Mother and Daddy said simultaneously.

We were all surprised at John. He was just coming down with flu and that probably explains it, but we didn't know that then. Also, whenever John gets hold of a subject that bothers him he worries it like Rochester with a bone until he's settled it to his satisfaction.

"I hate you, John," Suzy said.

"Why?" John asked. "It's carrying a premise to its logical conclusion." Then he relented and sounded more like himself again. "Look, Suzy, I'm sorry, but it's just silly to go on like this about Wilbur. I've been thinking and thinking about it, and it's just a place where we have to disapprove of nature and that's that."

"What do you mean?" Suzy asked stiffly.

"Yes, John, I think you'd better explain yourself," Daddy said.

"Well," John said, "we've been studying it at school this week. In nature every species lives by preying on another species. Every form of life lives at the expense of another form of life. We may not approve of it, but there's nothing we can do about it except die of starvation. So there's nothing for it except what Mother keeps saying the Greeks say: Moderation in all things. Suzy's not being moderate. She ate spaghetti last night with lots of meat in the sauce. And look at Daddy. Life's part of his job, but he can't go around feeling sorry for viruses—he has to do his best to kill them. I don't believe in

going out and shooting animals and things just for the fun of it;
I think it's an instinct gone wrong, from the days when people
had to shoot animals to get food to eat. And that's okay, where
it's a necessity."

"I don't want to talk about it," Suzy said.

"You're a horrid pig," Maggy said to John.

"If you call him a pig you're insulting Wilbur," Suzy said.

"Oh, for heaven's sake!" John took a large mouthful of
pork and applesauce and chewed disgustedly. Then he said,
"All I mean, Suzy, is if you want to be a doctor when you grow
up you have to stay alive to be one, and to stay alive you have to
eat a balanced diet. Moderation in all things!"

"Same to you, John," Daddy said. "You didn't need to get
Suzy so upset. That's not like you."

"I'm sorry, Suzy," John said, a little sheepishly. "I'll play a
game of checkers or Spite and Malice or something with you
before bed if you like."

But Suzy wasn't ready to make up. "I have an operation
scheduled on Pamela immediately after dinner," she said.
Pamela was one of Maggy's dolls.

So that was how the week began.

We wakened the next morning and it was a beautiful
morning. Among the most beautiful of the things we see from
up here on our hill are the clouds. It was a clear, sunny day, but
over the pines behind the graveyard enormous clouds were
tumbled, and more over the fields and mountains, great cold
masses of white and gray against the blue of sky.

We got off to school as usual, the dogs and two of the cats,

Hamlet and Prunewhip, following us down to the bus stop and waiting till we got on. And then at school, for no reason, everything seemed to go wrong. I made stupid mistakes in math and had bad papers to bring home. Maggy was sent to Mr. Rathbone, the principal, for being rude to her teacher. I had the same teacher once, so I could sympathize with Maggy, for a change. And when we got home from school John had been sent home from Regional because he'd thrown up, and he had a fever and was in bed with the flu. The guest room, which we were beginning to call John's room, is over the living room, and the piano is in the living room. I finished my homework, and Maggy and Suzy were playing checkers, and Rob was building a fort with his blocks, so I sat down at the piano to practice, something I don't particularly like to do, especially scales. So I started on scales to get them over with, and, I must say, I went at them with vim and vigor. I was so full of vim and vigor that it was quite a while before I heard a continuous thumping on the ceiling. I went up to John's room to see what was what.

"For heaven's sake, Vicky," he said irritably, "I have a headache and I'm sick. Those scales are going right through my head. Shut up!"

He said it so angrily that instead of being sorry for him I got angry, too. "I'm supposed to practice half an hour a day," I told him.

"Why don't you remember it on days I'm not sick, then? Mother's practically always having to force you down on the piano bench and hold you there. Why do you have to practice scales today?"

"Okay," I said, "so if I don't do well in piano this week, you can tell Mother why."

"Okay, I will," he said, and I stomped out. I stomped down the stairs and put on my red jacket with the hood and slammed out of the house. Behind the two birches the sky was a soft gold and it turned gradually to gold-green, and in the gold-green part, just between the two birches, was a tiny, silver-horned moon. Above the birches the sky turned to greeny-blue and there was one faint star just beginning to come out. It was cold and very dry, and I stood there and looked and shivered and shivered and looked. Then I came back into the house and sheepishly hung my jacket on my hook in the pantry.

And then everything should have been all right.

Daddy had called to say that he'd be late. The evenings Daddy is late we often eat at the table in the study and watch television, and Mother waits to eat with Daddy when he gets home. I helped her set up the table, and the little ones plunked themselves down on the floor to watch Mickey Mouse, and I went upstairs to read. I heard John go into the bathroom to throw up, and when he got back into bed I went in to him and said, "I'm sorry you feel awful, John."

He looked green around the gills and he stuck his face down in the pillow and said, "I'm sorry, too. I just heaved again."

"I know. I heard you."

"Did you tell Mother?"

"No."

"Well, why didn't you tell her?"

"I haven't exactly had time," I said. "I heard you and came in to tell you I'm sorry."

"When *you* throw up you want Mother to hold your head," John said. "I suppose it couldn't have occurred to you I'd like Mother to hold my head, too?"

John was sick; he had a temperature of a hundred and two. I knew I shouldn't argue with him, but, as I've said, it was just an awful week. Right from Wilbur the pig and Suzy's taking the gum and candy, nothing seemed to go right. And I've noticed that once you start doing things wrong you just kind of go on doing them wrong till something happens to make you stop. Sometimes I wonder if that isn't what makes people criminals. Nothing happens to make them stop, and they just go on doing things wrong till they get to be criminals.

So now I said to John, "You always seem to think Mother is your special property, just because you were born first. She's busy getting supper ready for me and the little ones."

"What about me?"

"You know perfectly well if you throw up you don't get anything but ginger ale and crackers. I'm going back down to practice."

"You're doing it just to spite me," John said. "Wait till I tell Mother."

"Mother doesn't like tattletales."

"Why don't you do something useful for a change," John said. "Why don't you do something to help Mother for once?"

John looked green, and I should have realized he was being cross because he was sick, but it wasn't my day, either, so I just snapped back, "Like what?"

"Just use your head, Victoria Austin. If you can't think of

something to do to help Mother, you're even dumber than I think you are."

"You think I'm dumb?"

"I know it."

"I'm in the top group in my grade."

"That doesn't prove a thing. You're so dumb you couldn't think of anything to do to help Mother."

"Oh, couldn't I?" I said. "I'll let the air out of the upstairs radiators, that's what I'll do. They were knocking last night and Mother said this morning she'd have to let the air out of them."

"Has she ever let you do it before?"

"She's never said I couldn't. Why shouldn't I?"

"It's on your own head," John said. "Go ahead, if you think you're so smart." And he pushed his face into the pillow and burrowed under the covers again.

Maybe I should explain about the radiators. We have hot-water heat. The hot water circulates through the radiators, and when air gets in with the hot water it keeps the hot water from circulating properly, and the radiators don't give off as much heat, and they make noises. We keep the upstairs thermostat lower than the downstairs one because we like to sleep in cool rooms and it saves oil, so the upstairs radiators seem to get air in them more often than the downstairs ones, where the water is constantly circulating most of the winter. Each radiator has a sort of little valve, and you take a key that looks like a very small roller-skate key and turn the valve, and hold a glass under the outlet. The air hisses out and you hold the glass there until a little stream of water flows into it, and then you know the air is out of the radiator. Mother keeps the upstairs key on her dressing table so it won't get lost, and I went and got it.

First I let the air out of the radiators in John's room, to annoy him. Then I did Mother's and Daddy's room, and then Suzy and Maggy's, and then Rob's and mine. I was doing the radiator by the north window and all of a sudden I felt the radiator key just turning and turning and I couldn't get it to shut off the valve at all. I took it out and a tiny sort of screw came out, and water came pouring out of the valve place and the outlet place, shooting out at the wall and the ceiling. There was absolutely nothing to do to stem the wild stream except put my fingers over the two places and hold. I was afraid the water might scald me, but I guess the little holes were so tiny that it didn't, because it didn't seem particularly hot, only very uncomfortable. I felt exactly like the Dutch boy with his finger in the dike.

"John!" I yelled. "John!"

"I'm trying to sleep," he yelled back. "Leave me alone."

"But a screw came out of the radiator!"

"I told you you'd make a mess of it. Go tell Mother."

"I can't! If I take my fingers away from the two little holes the water shoots all over the place."

"Serves you right," John said.

"Please call her for me," I begged.

"Call her yourself," he said. "I'm sick."

"But I can't! I can't move!"

Downstairs in the study the little ones had TV on, louder than Mother likes us to have it. I yelled and yelled and stamped and stamped for about five minutes before I could attract their attention. Finally Suzy came up to see what the matter was, and I told her, and told her to go tell Mother, quickly.

Well, she went back downstairs, and she says she meant to tell Mother right away, but she stopped off for a moment to look at TV and she got caught up in an exciting part of the story and just stayed there. And Mother didn't come and didn't come and finally I realized that Suzy couldn't have told her. So I began stamping and yelling again. It was the most awful feeling, being stuck to the radiator and not able to move. And I kept feeling more and more like the boy at the dike. I yelled at John again but he just laughed nastily.

Finally Mother came, and I was furious with John and furious with Suzy, and furious with Maggy and Rob, too, because they'd had the TV on so loud and been making so much noise, and I was furious with Mother for not having heard me and come sooner. I took my fingers away and the water came spouting out and Mother said, "Hold it again, Vic, while I phone Mr. Calahan," and she hurried off to her room and I heard her talking to Mr. Calahan, the plumber. Then she came back and said, "All right, Vic. Mr. Calahan will be over as soon as he can get here. Rescue us for a few minutes more, will you? Mr. Calahan says that if I get a potato and ram it up against the two little points where the water's coming out, it'll be a lot easier to hold the potato than the radiator itself. I'll go get a potato and then take over for you."

"John's a beast," I said. "He knew what was happening and he wouldn't call you for me."

"John's sick in bed," Mother said, "and I told him not to get out."

"He did get out. He went to the bathroom and threw up."

Mother looked at me quizzically. "Did you think I wanted him to throw up all over the bed? Now, hold it, Vic, and I'll be right back."

"And Suzy's a beast, too!" I shouted after her. "I told her to tell you right away and she didn't. Everybody just left me here to stew in . . . in radiator juice."

Mother laughed. "Just keep calm, honey," she said, and disappeared.

It didn't take her long to come back with the potato. I left her holding it on to the radiator and I went to the door of John's room and hissed, *"Beast."*

The phone rang, the house phone, and Mother called, "Answer it, please, Vicky."

It was for me, anyhow, Nanny, to ask me something about the Social Studies homework. She couldn't seem to understand what I was telling her about the assignment, so I said, "I'll get my bike and come over and show you."

"Is that okay?" Nanny asked.

"Why not? It won't take me long."

"But it's almost dark."

"I have a light on my bike and I'll go by the back road."

I knew perfectly well that it wasn't all right. John is sometimes allowed to ride on the main road, but none of the rest of us is. We can ride on the back road, but there're usually two of us, and it's never been after dark. But I didn't push thinking about whether or not Mother'd say yes if I asked her if I could ride over to Nanny's alone on the back road after the sun had gone down.

I went out to the garage, leaving all the warmth and comfort of the house behind me. As I shut the door I shut out not only the light and the sounds of the little ones watching television but my anger, too. Only now it was too late to turn back. I put on my jacket and pulled the hood over my head. It had turned very cold; I was sure it was below zero, and even with knee socks and my strong school shoes the cement floor of the garage seemed cold, and I knew the frozen ruts of the back road would be colder still, so I pushed my feet into my boots, though I've never liked riding a bike in boots.

You go downhill most of the way to Nanny's, then up a hill so steep that you have to get off and push your bike. I went in the back way, instead of going through the store. I wasn't quite sure why I didn't want her mother and father to see me, but I didn't. Nanny was on the lookout for me, and we slipped up their back stairs to her room. It only took me a couple of minutes to show her about the homework, so I said, "Well, I better be going. See you tomorrow in school," and I scuttled off.

I'd thought there might still be some daylight left, but in those couple of minutes it was all gone. It was really dark on the road now, and even with my strong bike light I didn't like it one bit, and I knew I'd been a fool to go tearing off to Nanny's in a rage like that. The sky was clouding over, deep masses of snow clouds, so there weren't even any stars. There are only a few houses on the back road between Nanny's house and ours, and great stretches of darkness in between. The back road isn't paved, and the dirt and ruts were frozen hard as iron, so that it was bumpy and uncomfortable to ride on. The shadows seemed enormous, and the distances between one house and another, between friendly lights spilling out of the windows onto frozen rusty lawns and the road, seemed much longer than I remembered. Finally I passed the last house and then there was about half a mile of pitch-black darkness before the end of the back road where it turns into the old Boston Post Road. Our house is on the corner. I pedaled as fast as I could. I forgot that I was mad at John, mad at Suzy, mad at anyone. All I wanted was to be home.

I'll never know exactly how it happened. Maybe I struck a rut or a pebble. Or maybe the hem of my skirt, which I'd torn that day at recess, caught in one of the pedals. Or maybe it was bicycling in boots. But whatever caused it, all of a sudden I was tumbling over the handlebars and onto a pile of rocks at the side of the road.

I didn't know at first whether I was hurt or not. I think maybe I was knocked out for a moment. I picked myself up and tried to get back on my bike to get home as soon as possible, but I couldn't ride it. My right arm hurt in a way that nothing had ever hurt before, and even if it hadn't, I couldn't have ridden the bike home because the handlebars were all bent around and the wheel was crooked. My face hurt, too, and when I put my left hand up to it, something felt horribly warm and sticky, and I knew I was bleeding. There was only one thing on my mind, and that was to get home as fast as I possibly could, and I started running up the dark road, and each step jolted the pain in my arm, and I felt the sticky warmth from my face trickling down my neck. For a long while I was too frightened to cry, and then, as I saw the lights from our house streaming across the lawn and I knew that everybody in there was warm and comfortable and *noisy,* I began to shriek. I didn't really know that I was shrieking; it just happened.

It was John who heard me, John who'd just had to get up to go to the bathroom and throw up again. He said he yelled out, "That's Vic! Something's wrong with Vicky!" And he flung himself into his slippers and bathrobe and dashed outdoors to the sound of my screaming.

When he got to me I must have looked just as awful as I felt. My face was all covered with blood, and it had dripped down all over my jacket. All John could say was, "Oh, Vicky, oh, Vicky," and then Rochester came bounding out, and he seemed to know that he mustn't jump on me, but he began to whimper and try to lick my fingers in comfort.

Maggy came rushing to the open door and took one look at me and ran back in again, screaming at the top of her lungs, "Aunt Victoria! Vicky's all bloody! Come quick!"

Then Mother came running out without stopping to put on a coat or anything. She took one look at me and said—and her voice sounded so calm I felt better at once—"John, you shouldn't be out of bed. Please get upstairs at once and take the little ones with you and keep them there till I tell you. Suzy and Rob and Maggy, go with John at once." They hesitated, and Mother said, "Now. At once. Before I count: one, two, three . . ."

They ran.

Then Mother put her arm around me and the protecting pressure of her arm came against my hurt arm and I screamed, "Mother, it's my arm! Mother, I've hurt my arm."

"All right, darling," Mother said. "Let's get indoors to the bathroom, where we can clean you up."

We moved slowly across the rectangle of light in which we had been standing and into the house. I couldn't move quickly. I had run all the way home, but I knew now that I couldn't run another step no matter what was after me. We went into the bathroom, and from the study the TV was blasting.

"Turn it off," I said. "Please turn it off."

Mother turned it off, then came back and turned on the water in the basin. Then she took a washcloth and began gently cleaning my face. "I think Daddy'll have to take a stitch or two in your chin," she said. "I'll call him in just a moment."

I turned so that I could see myself in the mirror, and then I screamed, "My teeth! Mother, my teeth!" My bottom teeth were all pushed in and bloody.

Mother said, very quietly, "All right, Vicky, don't be frightened. They can be fixed, don't worry. I'm going to try to get hold of Daddy now."

She helped me into the kitchen and I sat down at the table because I didn't think I could stand up any longer and now I was too frightened even to yell. I couldn't even breathe without a funny scared kind of sob coming up from my sides and choking me. Mother phoned the office number and got the answering service. She turned to me.

"Good. Daddy's at the hospital. I'll get him there."

Then she dialed the hospital number and asked for Daddy, and then it seemed to me she waited forever. Finally she said, "This is Dr. Austin's wife. One of our little girls is hurt." And then there was another long wait. She said, "Vicky, how did it happen?"

"I fell off my bike."

Then she said, "Oh, Wally. Wally, Vicky fell off her bike and I think she's broken her arm and her face is pretty battered . . . All right. Right away." And she hung up. "Come on, honey," she said. "We'll go down to the hospital and meet Daddy there. Let me just run upstairs and ask John to keep an eye on the little ones."

I was so stiff and wobbly that she had to help me into the car, and I sat very close to her, leaning against her. I could lean up close because my left arm was all right. What I really wanted was to be small enough so that I could sit in her lap and have her hold me, while someone else drove.

"Can you tell me more about it, Vicky?" Mother asked. "What were you doing out on your bike after dark?"

"I went to help Nanny with her Social Studies homework," I said. Then I added, very low, "I was mad at John."

Mother didn't say anything and we drove on in silence. She was driving quickly, more quickly than she usually drives, and as each minute passed, each thing about me that hurt began to hurt worse. My arm and my jaw particularly, but also it seemed that every bone in my body felt jostled and jounced.

Daddy was waiting on the steps of the hospital as Mother drove up. He helped me out and Mother went to park the car and Daddy took me down a long corridor. A nurse asked him if he wanted a wheelchair or a stretcher, but he said, "Thanks, we won't wait." He took me into a white room that was blindingly light, and helped me up onto a table sort of like the examination table in his office, but there was an enormous light over it. I began to feel all fuzzy and wuzzy, and Daddy said, "I'll have to sew up your chin, Vicky, but I think we'd better get some X-rays first."

All the rest of it I don't remember very well, and I'm just as glad. Daddy did get a stretcher and then I went up in an elevator, and then there were the X-rays, and the X-ray technician leaving me under the big X-ray machine and going into a little room and saying, "Don't breathe," and the buzz of the X-ray machine, and then, "Now breathe." And then I was in the elevator again and there was another doctor, Dr. Olsen, who's an orthopedic surgeon—that means bones and things—and Dr. Harlow, our dentist, and nurses and things, and Daddy said they were going to give me some anesthesia.

When I woke up I was in a room with one other bed in it, and I felt awful. My arm was in a plaster cast and I couldn't move my head at all and I couldn't speak. Daddy was there and I made some grunting sort of noises, and he told me to be quiet and lie still, and then he said that I'd broken my right arm and they'd set it, and he'd taken six stitches in my chin, and Dr. Harlow had put the teeth back in place, and to hold them properly he'd put a tongue depressor between my teeth, and then my whole head was bound up so I couldn't move my jaws at all. I felt thirsty and horrible and Daddy must have known this, because he took a spoon and dribbled some ice water into my mouth and I don't think anything has ever felt or tasted so wonderful.

Then Daddy said that he was going home, that John was sick, too, and he had to see to him, but that he'd come back down to the hospital later on to check on me, and that meanwhile I was to be good and not give the nurses any trouble. And he left.

I lay there and looked around the room. The other bed was empty and clean and white. The door to the room was partly open and light came in from it, but I couldn't move to look at my watch and they must have taken it off, anyhow. I didn't have any idea how late it might be. It was around five when I started home from Nanny's, and I didn't know how much time had passed since I fell off my bike.

Every once in a while a nurse or a doctor walked by, but no one came in. I wanted to cry out or to press the little buzzer pinned to my sheet, but I remembered Daddy's voice when he told me to be good and not give the nurses any trouble. My arm ached. My face ached. Tears started to come out of my eyes and roll down my cheeks but I couldn't sob aloud, not only because of what Daddy had said but because it would hurt too much.

And I knew it was all my fault.

This one I couldn't blame in any way on Maggy.

Only it seemed to me, as I lay there miserably, that before Maggy came to stay I'd never been as stupid and horrid and disobedient as I'd been that afternoon. Of course, that wasn't fair of me; I've been just awful lots of times when there wasn't any Maggy in our house. It just seemed that way. And I remembered a few weeks before hearing Daddy saying to Mother that Maggy was managing to disrupt the entire household, and Mother answering that if our household atmosphere was so precarious that a ten-year-old child could ruin it, it was a good thing to find it out. And Daddy said he wished Mr. Ten Eyck would make up his mind and just take Maggy back to New York. And Mother said that he was just as apt to decide to let her stay right where she was, with us; and if he did we couldn't refuse the responsibility; we had to give the child her chance.

I knew I couldn't blame Maggy for any of the things that I'd done that day. If I hadn't been mad at John, if I hadn't gone off on my bike in a huff, I might have been at home right that minute, maybe upstairs with Mother being read to or saying prayers. But I wasn't home; I was in the hospital, and maybe I'd made John worse, because he'd come running outdoors into the icy night air after me in only his pajamas and bathrobe. I wondered what Rob would say in his God Bless that night, if he'd ask God to help John get better, and to help me get better, too, and if he'd been scared when he saw me all bloody like that. Rob never seems to get scared at anything, but I think sometimes he feels things more than we know.

The longer I lay there, the worse I felt. And then a man's shadow stood near the door and then turned and came in. But it wasn't Daddy, it was Dr. Harlow. He came in and turned on the little lamp by my bed.

"Well, Vicky," he said, "how goes it?"

And suddenly I knew I was going to throw up. "I'm going to be sick," I said, mumbling through the bandages and the tongue depressor.

Quick as a flash he took out a pair of scissors and slashed through my bandages and stuck a pan out and I threw up lots of blood and stuff and he put his hand against my forehead to hold it till I was through.

"There," he said, "that was good timing, wasn't it? I'm going to bandage your head all up again to keep those teeth of yours immobilized, but not quite so tight this time. And your father and Dr. Olsen and I've left all kinds of pills for you to take and we want you to go to sleep, and sleep and sleep and sleep."

"I can't take the pills if you tie me up again," I mumbled.

"No, but you can take them *before* I tie you up," and he rang the buzzer on my bed.

A nurse came in and he said, "Bring in Vicky's medication now, if you will, please, Miss Dunne, before I get her all bound up again."

She brought me some pills in a little glass, and Dr. Harlow helped me to hold the water to swallow them with, because my unbound-up left hand seemed for some reason awfully shaky. Then he put the tongue depressor between my teeth again and tied my head up, turned out the light, and left me.

When he left me I started to cry again. I felt bad about crying because I knew Daddy wanted me to be brave and not give any trouble. Miss Dunne came in and looked down at me with a flashlight and saw the tears creeping down my cheeks, and she put her hand on my forehead, saying, "Try to go to sleep, Vicky, dear, and you'll feel better. You've been a good, brave girl, and your daddy'll be proud of you. Everybody's remarked on how cooperative you've been—Miss Fisher at X-ray, and Dr. Olsen and Dr. Harlow and everybody. So now you just try to go to sleep, and if you feel too miserable you ring your bell and I'll come in to you."

All I could do was nod, and she went out. I felt worse because she had praised me and it wasn't true, because I hadn't been a brave, good girl at all, I'd been awful to John, and I'd done something Mother would never have allowed me to do, and if I was hurt it was nobody's fault but my own—not Maggy's, not John's, not anybody else's—and the least I could do now was not scream and yell and make Daddy ashamed of me, too.

I closed my eyes tight and tried to pretend I was home in the big bed with Rob in the little bed at my feet, and that nothing hurt, that I was cozy and comfortable, and Mother would have to rout me out of bed in the morning to get ready for school.

I felt a shadow cross my eyelids and I opened them and Daddy was standing by my bed. He put his finger to his lips for silence. He laid Elephant's Child by me on the pillow and I knew Rob had sent his most precious possession down to me. Then Daddy pulled up a chair and sat down and took my left hand in his. He just sat there with me, not talking, holding my hand, until I fell asleep.

In the morning I wasn't sure at first where I was. Then I remembered. I'd never been in the hospital before, except to be born, of course, and John and I were both born in New York, though Suzy and Rob were born right here. Outside the windows the snow was coming down, big soft white flakes, tumbling over each other. And my arm ached and my face ached and I was thirsty. One of the nurses spooned a little soupy cream of wheat between my lips for breakfast, but it tasted awful and after a few bites I kind of gagged on it and she stopped. Dr. Harlow came in and looked at my teeth and bound me up again, but looser, and then Dr. Olsen came in and looked at my arm and said I was to have more X-rays, and I got wheeled down to the X-ray room and I didn't have time to think about home or Mother or Daddy or anything.

Right after I got back to the room, Daddy came in. I couldn't fling my arms around him because of my broken one and I couldn't kiss him because of my teeth, but he managed to give me a hug, and the first thing I asked him was when I could go home.

"Oh, in a few days if you're good," he said.

"How's John?" I asked. "Is he still sick?"

"He's kind of miserable," Daddy said, "but I think he's over the worst of his bug. But he's very upset about you, Vicky."

I looked at Daddy and didn't say anything. Finally I mumbled, "I'm upset about John."

"Why?" Daddy asked. I didn't say anything again, and Daddy said, "I know you don't feel up to talking much today, Vicky. Would you rather wait and discuss it later?"

I tried to shake my head, but that hurt worse than talking, so I said, "No, I'd rather get it over with."

"Get what over with?" Daddy asked.

"It was an awful day," I said. "I did everything wrong. I had a fight with John and it was my fault because John had a fever, and then when the radiator started squirting I got mad at everybody and I hated everybody, John most of all. And when Nanny called, Mother was holding the radiator, so I knew she wouldn't hear me if I left, so I got on my bike and I told Nanny it would be all right, but we both knew it wasn't, that Mother wouldn't have let me, so when I went to her house we sneaked up the back stairs and Mr. and Mrs. Jenkins never even knew I was there. Then I fell off my bike and I was all that way from home alone and it was dark and awful and when I saw the lights of the house I started to scream and John was the one who heard me and he came running out of the house to me. Did I make him worse, Daddy?"

Daddy never tries to pretend things, so all he said was, "I don't know, Vicky. But he isn't terribly ill; you needn't worry about him too much."

"Daddy!" I said. "What happened to the radiator when Mother left it to come out to me?"

"Your room and Rob's got pretty soaked, the wallpaper and the floor. Luckily, Mr. Calahan drove up right after Mother and you left for the hospital, so it could have been worse. The living-room ceiling's quite wet in one place, but he thinks it will dry out without leaving a stain. But if he hadn't come when he did and the water had gone on streaming out of the radiator, the whole ceiling might have fallen in. By the way, Vicky, who gave you permission to let the air out of the radiators?"

"I thought I was being helpful."

"Did you? Honestly?"

"I *thought* I thought I was."

Daddy said, "You managed to give yourself a punishment that was quite a bit rougher than anything Mother or I would have given you, didn't you? And remember, when you're hurt, Mother and I and the whole family are hurt, too. I've seldom seen your mother as upset as she was last night. You were a pretty horrible sight staggering down that lane. You scared John half out of his wits."

"Will you tell John I'm sorry?" I whispered.

"I think John knows that. He asked me to tell the same thing to you."

"Did Rob pray for me last night?" I asked, hugging Elephant's Child.

"Knowing Rob, can you doubt that he did?"

"What did he say?"

Daddy grinned. "He demanded very severely of God to make you get well quickly and come home and die of old age. Lie back, Vicky, and relax. You're going to need—and want— a good deal of sleep and rest for the next couple of days. Remember when Rob was about two? And we were all out in the orchard, and I was going on about something, a long speech about how the trees should be sprayed and pruned, and all about various kinds of sprays, and I paused to catch my breath, and Rob remarked loudly, 'Amen'? We all laughed, and it was one of his very first words."

I smiled, as Daddy had intended me to, though sort of weakly, sort of with my eyes and nose, if you know what I mean, because it hurt so to move my lips.

"Mother'll be down to see you during visiting hours this afternoon," Daddy said. "I've got to go now, Vic; I have other patients to see. Try to rest. Try to be good."

"I am trying," I said.

He held my hand firmly in his. "Yes. The nurses have all said that you've been a good girl, brave and not complaining. I

91

like to be proud of you, Vicky, and not ashamed." He bent down and kissed me, and left.

The funny thing was that I went to sleep almost as soon as he left. I woke up when lunch was brought in, and one of the nurses tried to feed me some soup, but I couldn't eat that, either. Some of the other doctors, friends of Daddy's and Mother's, stuck their heads in the door to say hello to me, but I didn't feel much like talking. I felt all kind of knocked out. I closed my eyes and kept going to sleep, not really a proper, good sleep, just kind of a gray doze, but while I was dozing I didn't hurt so much. Then I woke up and found Mother sitting by the bed. She'd brought down a book John had sent me, and cards the little ones had made me, and another book from Nanny, but I didn't want to read or even be read to. I just lay there holding Mother's hand and I kept wanting to cry, but I didn't. And I wanted again, as I'd wanted the night before, to be young and small enough so that Mother could pick me up and hold me in her arms and rock me the way sometimes she still rocks Rob because he enjoys so much being a baby.

She sat there and the snow kept on falling outside the windows, and I knew that as soon as the others came home from school they'd be out with the sled, and John would be furious because he couldn't get out on his skis.

And I was homesick.

After Mother left, it snowed harder. There was a light outdoors and I could see the snow falling against it, whirling and swirling wildly from both poles at once, and every once in a while I could hear a sharp crack as a weakened branch snapped off and fell to the ground. I knew that at home the ground in front of the house would be littered with twigs and branches from the elms; it always is when there's much wind. And the snow would sift in through the upstairs bathroom window right through the storm window. And in the morning the snow would be swirled into drifts and there would be patches of lawn blown bare. And I wouldn't be there.

One of the nurses brought me in some more soup then, and I thought of everybody getting ready for dinner at home and Suzy helping Mother fix a tray for John and trying to get John to pretend he was in a hospital and she was a doctor. But *I* was in the hospital, and Suzy, being under twelve, couldn't come see me, and it took every ounce of concentration I had not to cry while the nurse was feeding me the soup, but I didn't.

So that was the terrible week. I never want another week like that. And I don't suppose we'll ever know just why it happened, why we were all so awful and not the way we like to think of ourselves at all.

And Suzy still doesn't like to eat pig.

How Not to Have an Aunt in One Hard Lesson

In February, Aunt Elena had a break of two weeks in her concert tour, so she came to spend it with us. I still had my arm in a cast, but I'd got so I could manage dressing (except for tying my shoes) and eating and even doing my homework with my left hand. I could eat again, too, everything except very hard or chewy things, not fried chicken to pick up in my fingers or corn on the cob from the freezer. Uncle Douglas spent the first weekend Aunt Elena was here with us, too, and it was one of those weekends that come in February when it's warm and rainy, and you think maybe spring is just around the corner and start looking at the sharp branches of trees against the sky to see if they're beginning to soften with buds—but, of course, it's much too early. All the next week was like that, warm and moist and really unseasonable, and it got so muddy that it wasn't much fun to play outdoors, and the little ones kept coming in and tracking mud all over the kitchen floor.

Toward the end of the week Uncle Douglas called, right around dinnertime, when we were all in the kitchen. John was burning the trash in the fireplace because it was too muddy to go out to the incinerator. Suzy and Maggy were setting their part of the table; Mother was whipping cream; Aunt Elena was at the piano; and Rob was walking around talking to Elephant's Child. Elephant's Child is still his favorite thing in the world, and Mother and Daddy had put a new music box in it for Christmas. I answered the phone and Uncle Douglas said he wanted to come up the following weekend, that he was bringing up someone he wanted us all to meet, and could he speak to Mother, please.

Now, all the grownups are always thinking that Uncle Douglas is going to get married. And at least once or twice a year he brings up some girl or other, which must be awfully hard on the girl because we're all looking her over to see if we think she'd be a good wife for Uncle Douglas. Some of them have been very nice and we wouldn't have minded at all having them for aunts, and some of them have been just awful. Uncle Douglas's range of interest is very wide. But it seemed from the conversation he was having with Mother that this must be an extra-specially special girl, because he seemed to be worried about whether or not she would like us. And Mother said once, rather sharply, that we'd behave exactly as we always do, and if he was that worried about us, not to come up. Then she laughed and said, "I'm sorry, Doug, we'll do our best to be dignified and proper, but you know you yourself have anything but a sobering effect on the children."

Aunt Elena had come in from the living room and was

listening, too. She's very fond of Uncle Douglas and so Mother asked her if she'd ever met this girl, because Aunt Elena and Uncle Douglas have always seen a good deal of each other whenever Aunt Elena's been in New York.

"I don't think so," Aunt Elena said. "He seems to have had about half a dozen on the string lately. Does he really sound serious this time, Vic?"

"He's never been really worried about how we were going to behave before," Mother said.

"Oh, dear," Aunt Elena said. "If he wants you to be all proper and stuffy, she must be awful. We're all going to detest her."

Mother said, "Why do we react this way whenever Doug calls to say he's bringing up a girl? After all, we all keep saying how nice it would be if Doug would marry and settle down, and some of the girls he's brought up have been very nice. After all, Doug's twenty-nine."

"I was five when Daddy was twenty-nine," John said.

"I was two," I said.

"Jeepers," Suzy said, "Rob and I weren't even born yet."

Aunt Elena kept going on about Uncle Douglas's new girlfriend after Daddy had come home and we were all at the table. "If he's so worried that you won't behave, what on earth can she be like? Sounds like the kind who'd get annoyed when he gets paint all over everything and doesn't want his meals on time if he's in the middle of a picture."

"No matter what she's like, she can't be much worse than some of them," Mother said comfortingly.

Later that weekend I heard Mother saying to Daddy, "I'm

96

glad to have Elena taking as much interest in anything as she is in this new girlfriend of Doug's."

"Too bad Doug isn't older, or Elena younger," Daddy said. "They'd be good for each other."

"I don't suppose that would really matter in the long run," Mother said. "Anyhow, it's good for them just to be friends the way they are. But what about this girl? Do you suppose she's as bad as she sounds? It would really be pretty frightful if Doug married one of the creatures who've fascinated him momentarily."

"We'll have to wait and see," Daddy said.

Aunt Elena was talking about it again at the breakfast table, and suddenly John said, "Hey, Aunt Elena, I have an idea."

Mother said, "Whatever it is, I don't think I'm going to like it."

"Let the boy speak," Aunt Elena said.

"Well, Aunt Elena thinks she sounds so stuffy and as though she didn't have any sense of humor or anything. Let's find out. When we go to the station to meet her, let's all get dressed up in funny sorts of ways. Maybe we can borrow a few other kids so she'll think Mother's like the old woman in the shoe. And Mother can wear one of her old costumes and we can wear all our oldest clothes and look like ragamuffins."

"That won't be hard," Mother said.

"And Daddy can wear Mr. Jenkins's old raccoon coat and the big Alaskan fur cap Aunt Elena gave him. Then if she laughs and thinks we're funny she'll be okay, and if she takes it seriously or gets all stuffy about it we'll know she isn't and maybe we'll scare her off."

I never thought they'd do it. John told me later he never thought they would, either. What maybe did it was that Uncle Douglas called again, twice, to tell us that we must all behave over the weekend. Or maybe it was that Aunt Elena thought it was such a wonderful idea. She decided that she would be the maid, and began practicing a foreign accent for the part. So between Uncle Douglas calling and Aunt Elena taking an interest in something again and all of us teasing to do it, Mother and Daddy were talked into it.

"It really would be very good therapy for Elena," I heard Mother saying to Daddy.

And Daddy laughed and said, "You know you're just looking for a good excuse."

So Friday night we all got dressed up. We were really glad of the heavy clothes because the warm weather had vanished and the thermometer had plunged back down; from almost spring we were thrust back into winter. The wind blew from the east and sneaked its way in through all kinds of cracks and crevices we didn't even know existed. So warm costumes felt good. The four of us and Maggy made five children, and Daddy said that was plenty without borrowing any more. Mother went up to her costume trunk—and perhaps I'd better explain about Mother and her costumes.

That was how she met Daddy. Not in costumes or anything, but because she used to sing. Just the kinds of songs she sings to us at night, not grand opera or anything. During the war she went around a lot to the hospitals. Where there was a piano she played the piano, and had the men all singing with her. And where there wasn't, she played her guitar. She still plays it, not only for us, but at various club meetings and things like that, she'll go and sing for people. She met Daddy during the war at one of the hospitals. He was a doctor there, not a patient, but he was going through the ward once when she was singing and he stayed to listen and that's how they got to know each other.

Then, through one of the patients whose brother owned a supper club, she sang at the supper club for a while, and even though she only sang there one winter (because she married Daddy right after that) there was an album made of her songs, and we have it, and we save the records to play as a Special Thing whenever we're sick in bed. The costumes came from the singing, because as well as the pretty songs she used to sing, there were songs that were funny, too. No matter how sick I am or how high my temperature is, and it was a hundred and five once when I had flu, there's one song that makes me almost roll out of bed laughing.

So out of the costume box she got an old moth-eaten fur cape that came almost down to her feet. Underneath it she wore a red lace and sequined dress that only came down to her knees. She wore long earrings and false eyelashes and lots of makeup. Daddy wore a plain dark suit, but he borrowed the raccoon coat from Mr. Jenkins and wore Aunt Elena's enormous fur hat, and said he'd be the chauffeur. Aunt Elena went out and bought a brand-new maid's uniform. She was the only decent-looking one among us all—that is, from the neck down. From the neck up she didn't put on any makeup and she powdered her hair and she found a pair of glasses frames in

Mother's costume trunk and put them on and she really didn't look like Aunt Elena at all. As for us kids, we just looked like ragamuffins, and, as Mother said, that was easy. Rob wore red pajamas with the bottom hanging down, and Suzy and Maggy wore terribly old party dresses that needed ironing and had tears in them that had once been mine, the dresses, I mean, and were now too small for them, too. And John and I wore patched jeans and sweaters that were out at the sleeves. Of course, when we put our school coats on we didn't look quite as bad, but our school coats were all second-year coats this year so we all, except Maggy, looked shabby enough to suit Aunt Elena. Maggy kept jumping up and down and saying, "Oh, what fun! How do I look? Do I look pretty?" And actually she and Suzy both did look awfully pretty, Maggy with her straight shiny black hair and Suzy with her soft light curly hair, and the party dresses way up above their knees. It started to rain just as we left for the station, and Daddy said he hoped the rain wouldn't start to freeze.

The train was late and the rain kept on filming down and we all got terribly impatient. We played the Geography game till we ran completely out of A's, as we usually do, what with America and Asia and Antarctica and Abyssinia, and so forth, and we played I Packed My Grandmother's Suitcase and I Love My Love, and finally Rob cried out, "I hear it! I hear it!" and reached up his arms so Daddy could hold him up to wave at the engineer. The bell at the gate began clanging and then the train came round the bend, with its great eye shining and making a golden path with the rain slanting across it. Rob waved like mad at the engineer and the engineer waved back, and then

Daddy put him down and said, "Remember, Robert, I am just the chauffeur."

Uncle Douglas and Sally (he'd told us that's what her first name was) got off almost first. Uncle Douglas saw us. He was standing behind Sally and he put his hand to his head as though he were in agony, and then his eyebrows shot way up, and then he just shrugged.

Mother swept forward in her mangy cape and kissed Uncle Douglas on both cheeks, and when she spoke she sounded all la-de-da and not like Mother at all. "Doug, *da-a-h-ling*, we're so *enchanted* that you could make it! Wallace was detained, but perhaps he may be at home when we get there. And this is . . ." and she paused, archly, and held out her hand.

"Victoria, this is my friend Sally Hough. Sally, my sister-in-law, Victoria Austin. And these are her progeny."

We all danced around her, leading the way to the car. Maggy nudged Suzy and me. "I know that lady."

"What do you mean?" we whispered.

"I'm sure I've seen her somewhere. Maybe she was a friend of Mummie's or something."

"Stay in the background, then," Suzy whispered. "It would spoil everything if she recognized you."

Daddy was in the front seat of the car, with Aunt Elena beside him.

Mother said, "Of course you remember Grooves and Olga, Douglas?" She turned to Sally. "We're lucky to have such splendid servants in the back woods here. Grooves is *so* good at both chauffing and butling"—Uncle Douglas's eyebrows went up again, but still he didn't say anything—"and Olga is a perfect

101

jewel, aside from the fact that she's a *ghastly* cook. But she's *marvelous* at fixing the plumbing." We all piled into the station wagon, the five of us kids all over each other in back, and Mother and Uncle Douglas and Sally in the middle.

Mother, wrapped in her fur, said, "Grooves, open the window, it's stifling in here."

After a moment Uncle Douglas said, "I suppose you know it's raining in on Sally and me, Victoria?"

"Oh, is it?" Mother asked graciously. "You may raise the window an inch, then, Grooves."

Very carefully Daddy raised the window an inch.

Uncle Douglas said, "Grooves, shut the window all the way, please."

Daddy did not move, and Mother said, "Oh, I forgot to tell you. Grooves is a deaf-mute, but he gets my vibrations. Are you really chilly, Doug da-a-h-ling?"

"We will shortly be too frozen solid with an inch-thick casing of this rain to move from your car."

"These soft city people," Mother said. "But we mustn't forget our hospitality, must we? You may shut the window, Grooves."

Daddy shut the window.

"How long have you had this sterling couple?" Uncle Douglas asked.

"Of course, you haven't met them, have you?" Mother exclaimed. "We still had the O'Shaughnessys the last time you were here. But Olga and Grooves are such an improvement, don't you think, Doug da-a-h-ling?"

"A great improvement," Uncle Douglas said. "But almost anything would have been, wouldn't it?"

I don't know quite what we'd expected Uncle Douglas to do, but certainly not to go along with our gag the way he was doing. We'd thought we'd have fun and laughs at the station and then if we went on with it, it would all be just a joke, with everybody knowing about it. We turned up the road that leads to our house and Uncle Douglas exclaimed, "Victoria! What's happened to the great stone gateposts?"

"Oh, Doug, we're so distressed," Mother answered. "They went down in the last storm." Daddy let out an awful snort, then, but turned it into sort of a cough.

When we got back to the house Uncle Douglas sat back and let Daddy open the door and help him and Sally out, and Mother said, "You may take the bags to the blue and gray guest rooms, Grooves," and Uncle Douglas, instead of grabbing bags under one arm and children under the other, offered his arm to Sally.

Aunt Elena said, "I will unpack and lay your things out for dinner, Madam."

It was after nine by now, but Uncle Douglas always waits to eat till he gets to our house instead of going in to the dining car. Since it was Friday and John and I had brought home especially good school papers that week, we were to be allowed to stay up for dinner. When we got into the house Mother hurried upstairs with the little ones. Aunt Elena took Sally up to the guest room, which had never been called the blue room before, and Uncle Douglas went out to the gray room, also a brand-new name for the waiting room. John was going to sleep on the couch in the study.

We'd spent a long time that afternoon setting the table. Mother'd finally said we could use the best tablecloth, though she hates and despises ironing it, and we'd made it look as elegant as possible. Daddy was fixing something for the grownups to drink and Aunt Elena came down from the guest room.

"The girl's a snob to end all snobs, Wallace," she said. "She's inspecting everything as though she were from Scotland Yard and asking me all kinds of questions about the family that only an ultimate snob would dare to think she could get away with. How Doug ever got hold of her I'm sure I don't know, because I don't think she's ever been outside her own kind of people before. She's never met anybody like you the way you really are, much less like this. She hasn't the faintest idea what's going on."

"You mean she's taking it seriously?" Daddy asked. "Oh, come, Elena, nobody could."

"I don't think she's even stopped to ask herself whether or not she's taking it seriously. She looked absolutely stricken by the time I'd finished unpacking for her. And nobody told me there was going to be a snake in the guest-room dresser."

"I don't think that was supposed to be part of it," Daddy said. "Do you know anything about a snake, Vicky?"

"Well, John found a dead snake a couple of days ago," I said.

"Dead snakes do not belong in bureau drawers," Daddy said. "I shall have to speak to John."

"Well, maybe it wasn't John who put it in the drawer," I said. "He showed it to all of us."

"We were both too scared to scream," Aunt Elena said. "But

I carried it off beautifully. 'That's perfectly all right, Madam,' I said. 'He's a great family pet and hardly ever bites. As soon as he's through with his wee bit of a nap I'll get Grooves to take him to his bed.'"

"Your name is Olga and you talk about wee bits of naps?" Daddy asked. He handed Aunt Elena a glass. "Where's Doug?"

"Probably changing to white tie and tails in the gray room," Aunt Elena said. "Do you suppose he's furious with us?"

"We shall soon see," Daddy said.

Well, we didn't see right away, because as Uncle Douglas came in from the waiting room, Sally came down from upstairs. And Uncle Douglas took up the game right from where he'd left off.

"Well, Grooves, dispensing hospitality? How about one for me and Miss Hough, please?"

I wondered if Sally hadn't heard Daddy talking, but she just looked mildly shattered as she accepted the glass Daddy silently handed her. Now I had a good chance to look at her. I don't know much about clothes, but I knew enough to tell that hers were fearfully expensive, and not very becoming. And most of Uncle Douglas's girlfriends are young and pretty or, if they're older, then they're glamorous. Sally was certainly one of the older ones—she looked lots older than Aunt Elena— and there was nothing glamorous about her. She wore her hair like Mother, drawn back from her face into a knot at the nape of her neck, but while I think it looks beautiful that way on Mother (but maybe I'm prejudiced), it just made Sally look severe and cross and nobody you'd think Uncle Douglas could feel seriously romantic about.

Aunt Elena disappeared into the kitchen, and as soon as Mother came down, followed by John, Daddy went into the kitchen after Aunt Elena. Mother says Daddy has a noble faculty for always having a perfectly valid excuse for walking out on any situation that doesn't meet his satisfaction. I could tell Mother wasn't too happy with the situation, either. She accepted the glass Uncle Douglas handed her but she said, "If you two don't mind hurrying a bit, I really think we should get on into the dining room in just a moment."

"But, darling," Uncle Douglas said, "Miss Hough understands perfectly that you never eat before ten." Miss Hough, he called her. Yes, she was more like a Miss Hough than a Sally. "Or does the new couple like to get to bed before midnight?"

"Yes. By midnight, at any rate," Mother said. "Stuffy of them, isn't it? Servants are so difficult nowadays."

"But shouldn't we wait for your husband?" Sally asked, and we knew then that she really hadn't caught on to the game—she didn't know Daddy was Grooves or anything. I think she had a suspicion something wasn't quite on the level, but she didn't know what it was.

Mother blushed. She doesn't blush often, but John and I both saw her turn pink. And it was Uncle Douglas who answered, "Oh, he's probably off on a maternity case. Victoria will feed him when he gets home. I've seen her cooking bacon and eggs for him at three in the morning many a time."

There was an awful silence and I thought Mother was going to explain that the whole thing was just a joke, but Sally said, not in an approving voice, "Well, it's all certainly quaint, the house and the children and all the animals."

Daddy came to the door then and clapped his hands three times. "That means dinner is served," Uncle Douglas said, still taking over. "How becoming that dress is, Victoria dear. A new little number, isn't it? I must paint you in it."

"You have," Mother said. "Ten years ago."

Uncle Douglas's eyebrows shot up again. We all love his eyebrows, and Daddy's, too, of course, because they both have them, rather bushy eyebrows darker than their hair that can be raised (the eyebrows, I mean; this sentence seems to be getting kind of complicated) higher than you'd ever think eyebrows could go. They can also be lowered. When Daddy's eyebrows lower we know it bodes no good. Mother says no matter how difficult a patient is being, if Daddy lowers his eyebrows the patient behaves. I guess we're too used to Daddy to be frightened by it. I don't think he's ever frightened us, and I don't think he ever scares children, but some of his grownup patients are supposed to be terrified of him.

After Daddy had clapped his hands, Mother stood up and we all went into the dining room. The dining room is really part of the kitchen and it's one of the nicest rooms in the house. It's a wandery room, it goes in three different directions, because it's really several rooms knocked into one. Out the big windows we look down our hill to the village and then across to Hawk Mountain and the other mountains beyond. But now the curtains were closed and Aunt Elena and Daddy had lit the candles and the fire was blazing in the fireplace and Mr. Rochester was sleeping in front of it and Colette was asleep on her green velvet cushion in the red leather chair and looking perfectly beautiful; Mr. Rochester's beautiful in his big, brawny way, but Colette's glamorously beautiful, like Aunt Elena.

Sally said, kind of to make conversation, "Oh, what an adorable dog," and went up to Colette, and Mr. Rochester got up from his nap by the fire and went up to Sally and growled very softly, as though he thought she was going to hurt Colette.

Mother said sharply, "Rochester! Down! Go back to bed, sir!" And Mr. Rochester growled again, this time louder, put his tail between his legs, and stamped back to the fireplace. Yes, he did, he stamped. Even Mother and Daddy said afterward that that's exactly what it was like.

We all sat down at the table. Then a peculiar thing happened. We always say grace before meals. We have a special family grace that we say holding hands. And John and I looked at each other and when we talked about it afterward we found out that we were both thinking the same thing. We didn't want to say grace. Not with Sally there and Daddy and Aunt Elena hovering behind our chairs being a peculiar butler and maid. We weren't being us, any of us, and the people we were being weren't gracey people. Mother didn't make any move to start grace, either, and Daddy and Aunt Elena began passing the food, pot roast, which is one of the things that gets better if it has to sit and wait; Mother, being a doctor's wife, knows lots of those kinds of recipes. It wasn't the happiest meal we've ever had. It had all started out being so terribly funny and gay, but by now we were all feeling sorry for Sally, though we didn't like her a bit more than Aunt Elena had expected we would, and we were willing to do just about anything if it would save Uncle Douglas from her. She sat there eating her pot roast and her nose was one of those noses that always looks as though its owner is smelling something bad. Of course, you can't help the shape of your nose, but you *can* help its expression. Funnily enough, Uncle Douglas was the only one who seemed to be having a really good time. (He said afterward it's because he's a fatalist.) He kept asking Daddy and Aunt Elena, or Grooves and Olga, to pass us things. It was lucky they'd had something to eat with the little ones before we went to the station or they'd have been starved.

After we'd finished the salad, Uncle Douglas spotted a box of cigars a patient had given Daddy. Daddy doesn't smoke, so they were just sitting there, and Uncle Douglas indicated it, saying, "Pass the cigars, please, Grooves."

Daddy got the cigar box and handed it first to Sally, and she laughed her funny, whinnying laugh that didn't sound as though she thought anything was funny at all, and said, "Oh, how quaint! No, thank you." Daddy kind of shrugged and passed the cigars to Mother. Mother took one, bit off the end, and sat with it sticking out of her mouth, and this was really funny; both John and I almost burst into laughter, she looked such a riot sitting there in the crazy dress with the cigar between her teeth. She didn't light it, but said conversationally to Uncle Douglas, "I think I've about decided that I prefer cigars to chewing tobacco," and we knew she was trying to make it so absurd that Sally would just *have* to catch on. But Uncle Douglas took a cigar and Sally didn't say anything, though I'm sure she was beginning to suspect that it was more than just quaintness.

Mother had made a deep-dish apple pie for dessert, and

Daddy was just getting it out of the oven when the phone rang. It was the house phone, but often people will call the house number instead of the office number in the evening. Aunt Elena went to the counter and picked up the receiver and answered it. Then she turned to the table and said to Mother, "It's for Wallace."

Daddy, in his white apron, put the pie back in the oven, held out his palms in a well-what-can-I-do-about-it gesture, flung up his eyebrows, and went to the phone.

"Yes . . . Yes . . . Is the swelling underneath the jaw or just on the cords of the neck? . . . Temperature? . . . Yes, I think it probably is mumps, there's a good bit of it about right now, but I'll look in on him in the morning."

None of us looked at Sally while he talked. I think we were all glad it was over. It had gone too far—and that was partly Uncle Douglas's fault—and we'd all been hoping she'd help us out by catching on, and then she could pretend she'd known all the time and had just been playing along.

Daddy turned back to the table and said matter-of-factly, "Well, Sally, now we can all take off our costumes. I hope you enjoyed our little play. Doug's the best actor of us all. Is it all right if Elena and I sit down at the table?"

"You don't have to go out?" Mother asked.

"No, not for that. As you've probably realized, Sally, I'm Wallace, Doug's big brother, and Olga is Elena Huxley, one of our very dear friends."

I must say, Sally took it very well. She tried to laugh and say how clever we all were.

"Well, Sally," Uncle Douglas said, "since my family has

110

confessed all, don't you think we'd better have a double unveiling?"

"No," Sally said, with a warning shake of her head, and we wondered what on earth Uncle Douglas was talking about. I had a horrible idea that maybe he and Sally were going to announce their engagement, and if that was so, the longer they put it off, the better. Maybe Sally shook her head like that because after what had happened she didn't want to be engaged to Uncle Douglas. I hoped so.

John and I went up to bed as soon as we'd finished our pie. We walked Rob in his sleep into the bathroom, and then back into his own little bed at the foot of the big bed, and I felt terribly fond of him. Somehow it's often easier for me to feel terribly fond of Rob when he's asleep than when he's awake. I was too wound up to go right to sleep and I lay there listening to the sound of the rain against the windows. It was lashing against them and it sounded cold and icy and I was very comfortable under my pile of blankets and the big goosedown comforter. I heard the office phone ring and then the sound of Daddy's car going out of the garage, and I knew Mother always worried about him driving at night in bad weather.

I slept quite late in the morning. Rob's covers were thrown back and he must have dressed and gone downstairs. He has Saturday-morning farm programs he doesn't like to miss. He's apt to be up and downstairs earlier Saturday morning than any other morning in the week. I lay in bed and stretched comfortably with that nice Saturday-morning no-school luxury. It was a white, closed-in day, no mountains and only ghosts of trees.

The wind was blowing from the east, and not only the rain was pattering against the window but the wind was blowing the long, brown catalpa pods on the two tall catalpa trees constantly against the east windows and wall, a continual nervous knocking, an insistent but not very interested "Let me in!" It was a lovely morning just to lie there. So I did until I got hungry.

I went downstairs to get my breakfast, and toward the northwest a whole range of mountains was lost—simply vanished, as though the mountains had never been there. And fog was rolling across the fields with the rain, so that it was a sea of white. Sally had never been here before, of course, and it had been dark the night before, and I thought of all the things she could imagine under the fog instead of our gently sloping pastures and rolling hills: oceans and rivers and prehistoric glaciers, and castles and canyons and chasms—anything might be hidden, to be revealed when the fog rolled away. But I don't think Sally thought about things like that.

Everything looked raw and damp, and about the house things were *squeaking* (shutters, for instance) instead of *creaking*.

I was making myself some toast when the kitchen door opened and Daddy came in, looking tired, but kind of relaxed and happy.

"I heard you go out last night," I said. "Did you go out and come back again, or have you been out all this time?"

"All this time," Daddy said, "but it's okay now." I was glad. If things *aren't* okay, and, of course, sometimes they aren't, Daddy doesn't say anything but he acts quiet, and I can tell he's depressed and upset. Now he grinned at me and asked, "Any more coffee?"

"I'll pour you some," I said. "I've just made toast, too. Raisin bread. Want some?"

"Hand it over," Daddy said, and sat down in the red leather chair, shoving Colette off the cushion. She moved over enough to let him sit, then plunked herself down on his lap.

"Where's everybody?" Daddy asked.

"I don't know. I just got up."

"Victoria!" Daddy shouted, and Mother came in from the study.

"Wally! You'll wake everybody up."

"It's past ten," Daddy said. "Who's asleep?"

"Elena and Sally in the guest room, and Doug. What about your office hours?"

"I'm going right on down," Daddy said. "Just stopped in for a cup of coffee and a bite, which Vicky has very kindly provided. Also, thought you might mention to Elena that this rain is very likely going to turn to ice if the fog lifts, and it mightn't be a bad idea if she left on the early train tomorrow instead of waiting for the evening one if she really has to get back to New York. I'm not at all sure how good the roads are going to be." He finished his coffee and toast and stood up. "Well, be back for lunch. I hope."

All morning we could hear the rain and the catalpa pods lashing against the house. Mother said, "I think I'll fill the bathtubs, just in case," which she did, as well as filling several bottles with water and putting them in the refrigerator and the tea kettle and three saucepans. Sally came in looking sleepy and still as though things smelled horrid, and also looking just a little anxious, as though she didn't know what to expect next, and asked Mother what she was doing.

"Well, you see," Mother said, "the thermometer is reading right around thirty, and that means this rain is very apt to start freezing, and that means an ice storm. And if we have an ice storm, sooner or later the power is apt to go off. And if the power goes off, everything in this house goes off. We're run entirely by electricity. So we have no heat, we have no water, we have no stove, no refrigerator, no deep freeze, no washing machine, no dryer, no lights, no electric blanket—and really, I think Wallace and I miss that more than almost everything else!"

Sally blanched.

"And no television," Suzy said, coming in with Maggy, "and Mother can't play her records. And John can't run his electric trains. And if we had a sewing machine we wouldn't be able to use it. Mother, may we dress up?"

"Haven't you had enough dressing up for one week?" Mother asked.

"Couldn't we get the things out of the costume box in the attic?"

"All right," Mother said. "But make it *your* costume box, not mine."

Then Maggy, who, after all, was old enough to have known better, went up to Sally and said, "How old are you?"

"Margaret," Mother said warningly. "What have we said about personal questions?"

114

Maggy dropped that one, but she didn't take the warning. "Are you going to marry our Uncle Douglas?" she asked. "Because if you are, I want to warn you that his beard is very tickly."

"Maggy," Mother said in her quiet voice, "go up to your room, please, and stay there until you're ready to remember that you have manners. Suzy, you'd better go back in the study and watch television with Rob or John or do whatever they're doing until Maggy comes back down."

The rain didn't stop and the fog lifted and the thermometer stayed right around thirty. By lunchtime the black branches of the trees began to get a coating of ice, and the catalpa pods got coated, too, and the noise against the east windows was constant. Mother stayed in the kitchen, "cooking things against the storm." She made two pies and a big bowl of bread pudding with lots of raisins, and some tapioca, which Suzy and Daddy especially love, and lots of Jell-O for Rob. Daddy came in about one o'clock and said the roads were not good at all, and the road up the long hill from Clovenford, the same one we come up from the station, was beginning to ice badly, and he'd passed several cars that hadn't been able to make it, and he hadn't seen the sanding trucks out yet. They're always prompt in little Thornhill, but down in Clovenford, where the station and the hospital and Daddy's office are, they're much slower, partly because we have more ice up here than they do down in the town, I guess.

Saturday afternoon Daddy doesn't usually have office hours, but he went right back after lunch to make up some of the appointments he'd missed in the morning. John and I were both feeling sleepy, so we sat in front of the kitchen fire and read. I was rereading *The Secret Garden* and John was reading *The Sword in the Stone.* About five, Mother sent us to have baths, Suzy and Maggy and me upstairs, and John and Rob downstairs, and we were to fill the tubs again as soon as we were through. While we were in the tub the lights flickered and went off and then came on again. Mother came tearing up and told us to get out quickly and let the water right out and fill the tub again. Maggy said she hadn't washed yet, and Mother said that was just too bad, she'd had plenty of time to wash and she'd just have to stay dirty because those tubs had to be filled before the power went off.

Our tub was almost filled and we were about half dry when the lights flickered and went down, and then all the way out. And after a few moments the water stopped running.

Not only darkness comes when the power goes off, but silence, too. The perpetual winter purr of the furnace stops. Most of the time we don't hear the refrigerator, but when it goes off there's a strange silence. The deep freeze makes its noise, and whenever we run water the pump thrums away. The television wasn't on, but Mother was playing records, Schönberg's *Verklärte Nacht,* and that sighed off in the middle of a note. It was somehow a shock when the telephone rang and I remembered that it didn't depend on the Light and Power Company. It was the house phone and I ran to answer it in Mother and Daddy's bedroom. The house phone is on Mother's side of the bed and the office phone on Daddy's. I lay across the bed and picked up the phone and Daddy said, "Who's this? Vicky? I can hardly hear you, it's such a bad connection."

"Yes, Daddy."

"Tell your mother, tell Uncle Douglas, tell everybody, not to go out in the car. Period. The roads are glare ice. I'm at the hospital now and I'll be home when I can, and if it's not by dinnertime I'll call again, but tell Mother that whatever she's forgotten at the store, or whatever she's out of, she'll just have to stay out of."

"Okay, Daddy," I said. "Our power just went off."

Daddy groaned. "Wouldn't you know. Tell Uncle Douglas and John to help get the fires going in the fireplaces. I'm glad Uncle Douglas is there. Okay, honey, you help Mother with the little ones."

I gave Daddy's messages and Uncle Douglas and John lit the fires and Mother lit candles. The ice was beating against the windows and Rob stayed very close to Mother, holding on to her skirt, until she said, "Rob, darling, I love you very much, but I cannot move with you hanging on to me and there are certain things I have to do. All of you children sit in front of the fire and keep warm while I get the rest of the candles lit."

"Let's watch television," Maggy said.

"Let's play the Peter Pan record," Rob said.

"You can't do either," John said. "They don't work without electricity."

"Come on," Uncle Douglas said. "Let's sit down and feed the fires and I'll tell you stories."

We were in the middle of an exciting story about an Elizabethan pirate when I noticed Suzy wasn't with us. I looked around by candlelight and counted again. John and Maggy and Rob and I were sitting on cushions around the big living-room fireplace. Aunt Elena and Mother were wrapping potatoes in foil and putting them in the back of the fireplace. Sally was just sitting on one of the sofas. She and Uncle Douglas had been playing cribbage, and she had said she'd put the cribbage set away, but she was just sitting there. Her face flickered in firelight and candlelight, and where Mother and Aunt Elena looked beautiful to me, squatting in front of the fire and poking the potatoes back in the embers, the wavering shadows seemed to make everything long about Sally's face look longer, especially the nose. As a matter of fact, she looked rather like a witch, and I thought again how awful it would be if she married Uncle Douglas, and I didn't feel so bad about the trick we'd played on her the night before, especially as she hadn't even offered to help in any way when the lights went off. I wondered again where Suzy had gone to.

Suzy doesn't like to go to sleep unless her room is dark. She and Maggy have had several bad squabbles about whether or not the hall light should be left on till Mother and Daddy come to bed, and Suzy would really prefer not to have the night-light on in the bathroom, but all this is after she's safely tucked up in bed, and the night-light *is* on in the bathroom, and all she needs to do if she gets tired of darkness is to reach out and turn on the bedside lamp. Mother had candles in the living room and candles in the kitchen, and she had candles for us to take upstairs at bedtime, but we were never allowed to wander around with candles, and if Suzy wasn't in the kitchen she must be somewhere in the dark, and I wondered whether or not she was frightened.

•   •   •

Then I heard someone thudding down the stairs and I knew it must be Suzy and she came panting into the kitchen and I heard her demanding, "Mother, did you take my snake?"

"What snake, Suzy?" Mother asked. "I don't know anything about your snake."

Suzy stamped into the living room and over to where we were sitting by the fireplace. "Somebody has taken my snake. Who took it?"

"You mean that old snake I showed you?" John said.

"Yes. Did you take it, John?"

"I didn't do anything with it," John said. "I left it right on the stone wall where it was when I showed it to you."

"But I took it," Suzy said. "I put it in the bottom bureau drawer of the bureau in the guest room—your room. I knew you weren't using that drawer and Maggy made a fuss about having it in our room, and I thought it would be safe there. And now it's gone. I went to see if it was all right but it wasn't there." Suddenly she turned and glared at Sally. "Did you move my snake?"

"Wild horses wouldn't make me touch a snake," Sally said. "It was there last night."

"You mean you saw it?"

"I saw it indeed."

"Was he all right?" Suzy asked passionately.

Aunt Elena had come in. "We didn't examine him very thoroughly, Suzy darling," she said. "I was unpacking Sally's clothes and I really didn't think she'd want them on a dead snake, so after dinner I got your father to remove it."

"Remove it!" Suzy wailed. "But what did Daddy *do* with it?"

Mother came in from the kitchen now, too. "Suzy, what is all this? Why were you keeping a dead snake in the guest room?"

"To hatch!" Suzy cried.

Uncle Douglas was the first of us to realize quite how serious Suzy was. "Suzy," he said gently, instead of laughing as John and Maggy and I were doing, "how was it going to hatch? What was it going to hatch into?"

Suzy had started to cry. "Into a butterfly. A beautiful, big butterfly. You know, like a caterpillar. I know snakes must do something like that because last summer John showed me where a snake had left its skin on the wall, and I thought if I put it in the drawer where it was safe and quiet and dark it would be like a cocoon for it, and it would hatch into a b-but-butterfly." She was sobbing so hard now that she couldn't talk, and she ran and flung her arms around Mother.

Mother held her tight and stroked her head and said, "Oh, Suzy, Suzy darling."

And Suzy sobbed, "It would have been such a big and beautiful butterfly."

"Darling," Mother said, "the snake was dead. And snakes aren't like caterpillars. They shed their skins, but they don't weave cocoons or grow into butterflies."

"But it might have!" Suzy cried. "How do you *know*? It was a scientific speriment. Daddy says you never find out anything except by scientific speriments." And she began to sob again.

Sally said, "Oh, really!" And even if we'd thought Suzy was silly up to then, we stopped thinking it.

Aunt Elena said, "I know what, let's all sing!"

Mother had lit the two candles in the big silver candlesticks on the piano, and Aunt Elena sat down at the piano and started to play "Oh, Susannah," especially for Suzy, and Mother started singing, *Oh, Susannah, don't you cry for me,* and we all joined in, and then everybody was singing, one song after another— everybody except Sally.

"Why isn't Sally singing?" Rob asked.

"Maybe she doesn't know the songs," Mother said.

"Get your guitar, Victoria," Aunt Elena said, and Mother went and got her guitar and played along with Aunt Elena, and Uncle Douglas got the recorder he gave me for Christmas, which I wasn't very good at yet (he wasn't, either, but he had lots of fun with it), and Rob ran to the kitchen and came back with a saucepan for a drum. And Suzy forgot her snake. And we all forgot completely about Sally sitting silently on the sofa and not singing.

Daddy called around six to see how we were. The phone was really crackling by then, and I gave it to Mother because I could hardly hear him. She kept saying, "What? What? Shout louder, Wally!" And she was shouting at the top of her lungs herself. She said Daddy was going to stay at the hospital a while longer because some people had been brought in whose car had turned over on the icy road, and as long as Uncle Douglas was with us, he probably wouldn't get home till morning. We had a nice dinner anyhow, and Mother was able to stop listening with one ear for Daddy because she knew he wasn't coming home. "Unless they have some more emergencies, he'll probably have a better sleep at the hospital anyhow," she said, "and heaven knows he needs it."

She'd brought steaks up from the deep freeze and we cooked them over one of the fires, and there were the potatoes she'd baked in foil, and she'd made a big salad, and we ate on paper plates because, of course, there wasn't any water to wash dishes with, and it was all like a picnic and fun. At least, we children had fun, and Mother and Aunt Elena and Uncle Douglas seemed to be enjoying themselves, too.

But once, when all the grownups, even Sally, were out of the room, Maggy whispered, "I know I've seen her before, that Sally Hough. I know the name, too, but I can't think where."

"But *think*," Suzy demanded.

"I've been trying. She must be one of Mummie's friends. And she keeps on looking at me as though she knew me, too. I don't like her."

None of us did.

We were already in our nightclothes, and Mother said we'd forget about brushing our teeth for one night, and then she had us all go to the bathroom, one after another, and then she took a bucket and filled it with water from the tub and threw it down the toilet, and that made the toilet flush. Rob was fascinated and wanted her to do it again, but she said he'd have to wait till morning.

It was Rob's and my turn to have prayers in our room. Mother left a candle burning on the bureau in the little girls' room (they *don't* like being referred to as the *little* girls but, after all, I'm three years older than Suzy and two years older than Maggy) and she put a candle on the highboy in Rob's and my room and another candle on the bed table so she could read to us. A room looks very different by candlelight than it does by electric light. Our house is almost two hundred years old, and in winter, even with storm windows, there are drafts that get in at odd places. So the candles would flicker and flare up into long thin orange streamers of flame with a tiny bit of purple smoke curling up beyond, and then the wind would miss its crack and the flames would settle down to fat yellow glowings. By electric light I don't notice shadows very much, except when we play shadow games with our fingers, making rabbits and faces and things on the wall (Daddy and Uncle Douglas are the best at it). But when the candlelight flickered, the shadows moved and changed shapes. Sometimes the shadow of the lamp on the desk would be short and squat and sometimes it would seem to fly up and streak halfway across the ceiling.

Mother read to us, and then we said prayers. Rob asked God to help make the electricity get better and then he did all the family God Blesses and then he said, "And Sally—and Sally—oh, well, God, I s'pose you'd better bless Sally, even if we don't want her for an aunt. And, God, please don't let that moth on the ceiling eat my clothes. And bless me and make me a good boy. Amen."

Mother brought her guitar and sang to us as a special treat. It had begun to get kind of cold upstairs by this time, since there aren't any fireplaces to help keep it warm. There were all those radiators and not a bit of warmth in any of them, and we never even think of them unless they stop working. Mother heaped extra blankets on all of us and went downstairs.

In the morning, even with all the blankets over me, I could tell that upstairs was really cold. My nose was about the only thing poking out of the covers and it was icy. I looked down at the foot of my bed to Rob's little bed, and I couldn't see him at all, but I knew he was in there because there was a mound of covers sticking up. The east window was completely coated with ice; you couldn't see out at all. But you could hear that the ice was still beating against it, sharp and cold.

When Mother comes up to bed at night she puts out our clothes for morning. She had put out ski clothes for us, warm outdoor clothes, and as I got up and dressed I knew we'd need them. When I was dressed I fished Rob out from under the covers and dressed him quickly, and we ran downstairs.

John and Uncle Douglas were feeding the fires and Mother had managed to make instant cocoa for us in the big fireplace. Aunt Elena had bread on a long fork and was toasting it for Suzy and Maggy, who were already down. Sally had not yet appeared.

When I looked out the south and west windows I could see that the rain had stopped falling. It was ice falling from the trees, from the roof, that I had heard hitting against the windows. There were lots of little branches and quite a few big ones from the elms on the ice-covered lawn. A big branch was split off the oldest and loveliest of the apple trees down in the orchard. And out the kitchen windows I could see that the two birch trees were bent all the way down to the ground in two iced arcs, and the little pines we put in last summer were all bowed down with ice.

We didn't sit around the table for breakfast, but stayed at

the big fireplace in the living room. Aunt Elena said to Mother, "Now, look, Victoria, I couldn't be happier than I am here, ice or no ice, marrow congealed in my bones or no, but as you know, it is imperative that I get back to New York tonight. Wally suggested that I take the early train. What about it?"

Uncle Douglas said, "And since Sally feels that she has accomplished her mission in coming here, we might as well go down on the early train, too."

Accomplished her mission? What did Uncle Douglas mean by that?

Aunt Elena put her hand on his knee and said, "I'm sorry, Doug. It was really my fault."

And John said glumly, "No, it was my idea."

"It was nobody's fault," Mother said briskly, "and nobody can foretell the final results. As for the early train, the roads aren't bad today. They've been sanded and it isn't raining any more."

"But if everybody goes at once," Aunt Elena said, "it'll mean that Victoria has to drive home from the station alone, and I don't think Wallace would like that."

"I won't be alone," Mother said. "I'll have five children with me."

"And if Sally had her way, it'd be four," John muttered in my ear.

"What on earth is all this——" I started.

John said, "Shush, I'll tell you in a minute," and then the phone rang, a funny sort of squawk, not a proper ring at all, and Mother got up to answer it. She kept shouting, "I can't hear you! What? What?" and finally she gave up and hung up.

"That was Wallace," she said. "At least, I think it was. I didn't get a single word, but the voice sounded familiar. And I don't think he heard me at all. Okay, Doug and Elena. If you're going to go I think we'd better get ready. We need to give ourselves twice as much time as usual, though I'm sure the trains will be running late. Elena, you'd better go upstairs and wake Sally. Children, get your beds made, please."

John said, "Vicky, come help me with mine and Uncle Douglas's, and I'll help you with yours and Rob's." We went into the study and John said, "Now, you must promise not to say anything to the little ones, because Mother doesn't want them upset, but she said I could tell you."

"Tell me what?" I demanded. "What is all this?"

"I came down early this morning," John said, "and it was just Mother and me building up the fires, and she told me what happened last night."

"But *what* happened?"

"Hold on, I'm trying to tell you! Well, you see, Sally isn't Uncle Douglas's girlfriend at all."

"What a relief! She isn't? Whose girlfriend is she?"

"Nobody's, as far as I can guess. She's Mr. Ten Eyck's niece. She's a cousin of Maggy's."

"Of Maggy's!"

"Yes. That was why Maggy knew her. She'd met her at her grandfather's."

"But if she's a cousin of Maggy's, what was she doing here, and with Uncle Douglas?"

"That's just the point. She was inspecting us for Mr. Ten

126

Eyck, to see if we were fit people for Maggy to stay with. And Sally decided that she could inspect us better if we didn't know who she was or why she'd come."

"What a dirty trick!"

"Well, sure, but I see her point."

"We fouled it up all right," I said, and wondered why I wasn't gladder.

"Yeah. We sure did. Uncle Douglas said he never thought we'd *really* think she was one of his girlfriends. But I guess he doesn't realize that she isn't any more peculiar than lots of the others he's brought up. And, of course, he couldn't have known we'd come down to the station looking like that."

"But why did he play along with the game?" I demanded. "Why didn't he just stop it right away?"

"That's what Mother and Aunt Elena asked him. But he said the damage had already been done, with us arriving at the station looking like that, and it was the only way he could see to make the weekend any fun at all, and he hoped all along that maybe Sally would turn out to have a sense of humor after all."

"But she didn't," I said, yanking John's top sheet straight.

"No. I think it was Suzy's snake that finished her. I guess she was pretty awful to Mother and Aunt Elena and Uncle Douglas last night. She wanted to take Maggy right back to New York with her today. She said that if Mr. Ten Eyck couldn't take her, then she'd offer her a home herself."

"So I guess Maggy won't be with us much longer," I said.

John pulled up the blankets and pounded at them sort of absentmindedly. "Looks that way. Are you glad?"

"Not as glad as I thought I'd be," I said.

127

"Neither am I. I think she's sort of changed in the last few weeks. I mean, she's more like just any other little girl instead of being so—so ubiquitous."

"Ubiquitous" is one of John's pet long words and it's a good one for Maggy. It means being everywhere, or sort of seeming to be all over the place at the same time. And that's how Maggy did seem. There always seemed to be more of her in the house than the four of us put together.

"I guess I'm really sorry for her now," I said. "I wasn't at first. But I am now." And it was true. Now I could empathize with her.

"It's like sending her to the lions," John said. "Can you imagine what it would be like to live with Sally? Jeepers, Vicky, we *should* have known right from the start she couldn't have been one of Uncle Douglas's girlfriends! Uncle Douglas's really goofed on some of them, but Sally just isn't his kind of goof."

"But even Mother and Daddy didn't guess about her," I said. "Oh, *poor* Maggy! I mean, we aren't perfect, but it's always pretty nice around our house."

"I'll feel kind of awful if it's all because of my idea she gets sent away," John said.

"I don't think Sally would have approved of us anyhow," I tried to comfort him. "There'd have been the snake, and the power going off."

"We couldn't help the ice storm!" John was indignant.

"I'm sure Sally thinks we could. And we're always noisy. And she didn't like it when we all sang."

"Well . . ." John said. And then, "Uncle Douglas says that he feels that certain things are meant, and what's to be will be about Maggy, no matter what Sally says to Mr. Ten Eyck."

128

"I wish Uncle Douglas and Aunt Elena could get married," I said. "Then Maggy could live with them. That's what Maggy's father wanted, anyhow, for her to be with Aunt Elena."

We finished the beds and then went into the kitchen. Uncle Douglas was saying to Mother, "Victoria, you are undoubtedly the worst mother in the world, but I love you anyhow."

And Mother got kind of indignant and said, "Come, now, I don't think I'm all that bad."

And Uncle Douglas gave her a big hug and said, "You can be the mother of my children if you like."

Mother laughed and said, "That would hardly be proper," and then Aunt Elena and Sally came into the kitchen, dressed to go, and Aunt Elena said, "Go see what's looking coyly in the bathroom window."

None of us had been in the upstairs bathroom that morning, since it was so cold upstairs, so we all ran up like a small herd of elephants, and there, stuck right through the frozen screen, peered the television aerial!

Just before it was time to leave for the station I went into the hall toy closet to find something for Rob, and Sally drew Maggy away from the others and into the study. I could see them and hear them from where I was in the hall, and I have to admit right here and now that I just stayed and listened. I didn't actually eavesdrop, I just happened to be where I could hear. Or, let's face it, I guess it *was* eavesdropping, and I guess it was wrong, but I'm glad I didn't go away as I ought to have done, because it made me feel lots closer to Maggy.

"Margaret, dear," Sally said, "don't you recognize me?"

"I think I know you," Maggy said cautiously, "but I'm not sure who you are. Are you one of Mummie's friends?"

"I'm your mother's first cousin. I'm your Cousin Sally."

"Oh," Maggy said flatly.

"Aren't you glad to see me?"

"I don't know you very well," Maggy said. "And if you're my cousin, why didn't you tell me before?"

"I wanted to see how you were getting on, and if you were happy. Margaret, dear, wouldn't you like to come live with me?"

"No," Maggy said, and she didn't add "thank you."

"But you know, dear, I'm your closest relative now, after your grandfather."

"I don't know you nearly as well as I do Aunt Victoria and Uncle Wallace, or Aunt Elena and Uncle Douglas."

"They aren't your real aunts and uncles," Sally said. I thought that was awful of her.

"They feel lots realer than you do," Maggy said.

"Time to leave now," Mother called just then.

We all piled into the station wagon and Mother drove us down to the station. Sally sat in front between Mother and Aunt Elena and hardly said a word. When we got to the station we found out that the train was going to be quite late, but the station was open and warm, and the electricity hadn't gone off down in Clovenford, so we left them sitting there to wait.

In the car on the way back up the hill Mother said, "Well, children, that will teach us to play practical jokes. They're almost always like boomerangs; they come back and hit you in the face."

"But we didn't like Sally, any of us," Maggy said. "It would be awful if she married Uncle Douglas." I could see, then, why

Mother hadn't wanted the little ones to know who Sally was. Luckily, I don't think Maggy realized that Sally might be deciding her fate. I think she thought Sally really was Uncle Douglas's girlfriend; and just because she'd told Sally she didn't want to live with her, that would be the end of that. But I was afraid for her.

So we drove home. The roads were sanded and the car got covered with sand and the windshield splashed with mud so that the windshield wipers didn't do much good. The trees down in Clovenford weren't all iced, but just before we got back to Thornhill they started to be sheathed again, and we could see wires down all along the roadside and the Light and Power trucks working on them. Mother slowed down and asked one of the men when he thought the power would be back on, and he said, "Don't ask me, lady, but don't look for it before tomorrow."

During the afternoon the wind shifted, swinging around from the southeast to the northwest, and the thermometer dropped down to a shivering ten degrees. Even when the furnace is working full time the house is coldest when the wind is blowing hard from the northwest. Mother stationed us in front of the fireplaces and we kept putting logs on and as long as we stayed right close we weren't too cold. Mother began to worry about the pipes, and she and John went upstairs and draped blankets over the radiators to try to keep them from freezing. The office phone rang once, but when we went to answer it, it was completely dead.

Have you ever noticed how things *look* different when it's terribly cold? I don't think it's imagination to say that things look harder—the grasses and small trees especially. And things don't have as much color, they fade. Uncle Douglas says that this is observant of me, and absolutely true. And then there's the feel, the cold against your face as though your skin had been turned to polished metal. And I always feel, for some reason, terribly clean when it's specially cold. And all kinds of wood, trees, and the wood of the house creak and crack in protest.

About six o'clock Daddy walked in, and we all rushed at him and tried to climb up on him, until Mother shouted, "Children! Daddy's tired! Leave him alone!" And she sent us all to sit in front of the fireplace in the kitchen while she got dinner at the fireplace in the living room, and John and I knew she was telling Daddy about who Sally really was and everything that had happened.

We all went to bed early because in an ice storm that's the coziest, warmest thing to do.

I don't know how long we'd been asleep when I felt someone shaking me, and I opened my eyes and it was Mother, holding a flashlight. "Put something warm on, Vicky," she said, "and come downstairs and see fairyland."

I put on my bathrobe and fuzzy slippers and wrapped a blanket around myself and ran downstairs, and so did everybody else. Daddy had Rob rolled up in a blanket and was carrying him, which pleased Rob very much. We looked outdoors and the moon was high and full and it streamed through the trees and every single tiny twig was cased in ice and shimmered like diamonds. And the ground shimmered, too, because it was covered with spangles of ice. The two birches were twin shining arcs of ice that seemed to be spraying off rays of light. As the wind shook the trees tiny bits of ice would break off and catch the moonlight as they fell to the ground. Little clouds scudded across the moon, and it made the moon look as though it were flying across the sky; and then the trees made long delicate shadows that came and went along the icy ground. It was so beautiful we couldn't speak, any of us. We just stood there and looked and looked. And suddenly I was so happy I felt as though my happiness were flying all about me, like sparkles of moonlight off the ice. And I wanted to hug everybody, and tell how much I loved everybody and how happy I was, but it seemed as though I were under a spell, as though I couldn't move or speak, and I just stood there, with joy streaming out of me, until Mother and Daddy sent us up to bed.

And I lay there in the dark and I was absolutely positive that God would not allow Maggy to be thrown to the lions.

The next morning the house was bone-cold, and not being able to run water and having to cook over the fireplace had lost its glamour. Rob was kind of whiny, and all of us felt a little cross. Mother said something to Daddy about sending us all somewhere where there was a coal furnace and we could warm up, but Daddy said that the power just had to come back on soon.

After breakfast we burned the paper plates and napkins and things, but even so the sink was full of the pots and pans Mother had had to use and hadn't been able to wash, and the whole house looked cold and kind of grimy. Daddy and John brought in loads of wood and stacked it by the fireplace.

Then, suddenly, all over the house, lights clapped back on,

and there was a sudden whirring and buzzing of noise as all the motors started, and we could feel the furnace throbbing in the cellar! Oh, what joy, what joy! We ran all over the house turning lights off, and then turning them on again, just to make sure they really did work. The water in the upstairs bathtub began to run as soon as the pump filled up the tank, and I turned the tap off and then just stood there and listened to the lovely banging of the pump and the thrum-thrum of the furnace and the rattle of the deep freeze. In the kitchen in short order Mother was doing dishes, doing one load of wash and drying another, and then she went to the vacuum cleaner, flying through the house putting it in order again, with the phonograph on full volume, loud cheerful music, Handel's *The Cuckoo and the Nightingale*. Gradually the house began to warm up and we started shedding sweaters and jackets. The office phone began to ring, so we knew the phone men were out working, too, and things were back to normal. Then the house phone rang, and it was Uncle Douglas, and he said, "Be of good cheer, little Vic. When Sally told her horrendous story to Mr. Ten Eyck he roared with laughter, so I think our little Maggy's safe for a while longer, at any rate. Now let me speak to your mother."

I gave Mother the phone, and then I rounded up all the kids to play a game of hide-and-seek, because I was so happy I had to take it out in some kind of romp. And even two days before, if anyone had told me I'd be wild with delight because Maggy wasn't going to leave us, I don't think I'd have believed it!

The Anti-Muffins

Every once in a while something happens to make you realize you don't know someone you thought you knew inside out. My brother John, for instance. John's always been my big brother, and I've admired him and loved him and hated him and fought with him and never thought much about him, simply because he's just John.

And our father. Daddy's a country doctor, and he's familiar and safe, and it's hard for us to realize that lots of people are afraid of him.

And Mother. She's just Mother to us, and that's enough.

So of course the John we see isn't the John anybody else sees, and that's a big thing to realize.

It started out with measles. All in one week John and Maggy and Suzy and Rob came down with measles, in chronological order.

I didn't, heaven knows why. So I helped Mother take care

of the others because she said there wasn't any point in trying to isolate me; I was already thoroughly exposed and I might as well make myself useful. This mostly meant taking care of Rob.

Everybody was miserable, everybody had a high fever, but Rob was the most miserable of all. His head ached and his eyes hurt and every part of him was uncomfortable, and any time Rob is hurt or sick he believes in letting everybody know about it. So this time he thought he was much sicker than the others, and Daddy said he was, a little, but not nearly as much as he thought he was.

John lay in the guest room with Rochester by his bed, when Rochester could be called away from Rob. Mother put up the dart board on the wall across from John's bed and he threw darts. And then he played records. He played Mother's records, and his album of country-and-western, and Mother said if she heard *The Gambler* one more time she'd break the record over his head, measles or no. He wanted to watch television, but the TV is downstairs and Daddy said it wasn't good for his eyes, which are a bit weak, anyhow. We seem to watch a lot less television than most of our friends, partly because our parents limit our watching, but largely because there's so much else to do.

Daddy brought home two small dolls for Maggy and Suzy and they lay in bed and played with the dolls and slept and complained. Suzy pretended both the dolls had smallpox and she was a famous doctor taking care of them during an outbreak of smallpox because, she said, people got careless about vaccinations, and it was a new strain. And she had Maggy's doll die of smallpox, and then Maggy shrieked and yelled and screamed herself to a pulp, and Mother said Suzy would have to invent a new serum to resurrect Maggy's doll, and Suzy felt mean because she was sick, and she said the doll was dead and she was going to perform an autopsy, and Maggy leaped out of bed and grabbed Suzy's doll and pulled off one of its arms and they started to have a free-for-all, and Mother had to send Suzy into her and Daddy's bed to wait until Daddy came home.

And Rob just felt miserable. Mother was so busy with the others that I stayed with Rob. I drew the curtains at the windows and got my big soft quilt and rocked him and sang to him and told him stories, and Colette cuddled with us, too, and I discovered again how terribly much I love my bratty little brother.

So everybody got over measles and went back to school. The incubation period went by, and Daddy said, "Well, Vicky, it looks as though you have a natural immunity to measles."

But the next day in school my head began to ache, and my eyeballs began to throb, and if you've never had measles you haven't any idea how awful you feel. So about eleven o'clock my teacher called Mother, and she and Rob got in the station wagon and came over and brought me home. Mother said, "Well, Vicky, it looks as though you weren't immune to measles after all, but you certainly waited till beyond the last minute to get them."

I undressed and Mother turned down my bed and when I got in the sheets felt cool, and the pillow soft and good to my head. Rob brought me up a glass of ginger ale, and that tasted just perfect, and I felt quite cozy and contented. But then my head began throbbing and my eyeballs hurting and the pillow was hot and the bed had lumps and the sheets instead of feeling smooth were suddenly scratchy, and I realized how good Rob had been while he was so miserable. And I was lucky because I was the only one who was sick, so Mother could pay more attention to me. She sat by the bed and stroked my head with cool fingers, and Rochester flopped down by the bed as much as to say he'd take care of me, too. When the others got back from school they came in and said they were sorry, because they knew how miserable I felt, and Suzy fixed my bed, straightened the sheets and turned the pillow so it felt cool again. When John got home from the Regional High School he said I could have the dart board; he'd put it up for me, but I didn't feel like throwing darts. I didn't feel like watching television. I didn't even feel like listening to Mother's records, so I knew I was really sick.

Rob went into the guest room with John that night so I wouldn't disturb him with my tossing and turning and my feverish bouncings, and so he wouldn't disturb me if he snored. But I was used to having Rob's small bed at the foot of my big pine bedstead. I didn't want him to go. I cried and that made my eyes worse. John came in to say good night and to bring me aspirin, and said, "I guess I was just lucky and didn't have it as bad as you, Vic. Even with my myopic eyes my head didn't ache much after the first day. Maybe you'll feel like playing darts or something tomorrow. I don't suppose you'd like me to set up my electric train in here where you can see it?"

John's electric train used to belong to Uncle Douglas, and it's got all kinds of cars and bridges and tunnels and bells and whistles and the thought of all the noise made me shudder, but

I tried to be nice about it because he meant it kindly. I hoped he wouldn't offer to reconstruct his space station for me.

I felt very sorry for myself. I thought it would have been much more fun to have had measles with everybody else, and if I'd had it then I wouldn't have been so sick; and Daddy wasn't home that evening and I wanted Daddy, and I resented Mother spending time with the others at bedtime. It was really rather nice while everybody else was sick and I was taking care of Rob, but it was awful with me being sick all by myself and everybody else feeling fine.

I tried to go to sleep but I kept bouncing around and the sheets got all messed up again and I needed Suzy to fix them, and the aspirin didn't seem to have helped at all. The hall light was on and a shadow moved across it, and then John was standing in the doorway. "It's me again," he whispered. "Are you still awake?"

"How could I sleep when I feel so awful?" I asked. Maybe I was good when I was in the hospital after my bike accident, but I wasn't good about having measles.

"Mother wants to know if you want some more ginger ale."

"I guess so."

He was back in a moment with a cool, amber glass, and I rose up on one elbow and sipped at it and began to feel a little better. The light coming in from the hall was just enough light not to hurt my eyes, and John was standing there by the bed looking sorry for me, and that helped, too. John has a way of making people feel that he cares what happens to them; that's one of the nicest things about him, because it's true. He really does care.

"I've been out walking around the orchard," John said.

"It's late."

"Not that late. Just about eight-thirty, and it isn't even quite dark around the edges. It'll be summer before we know it. The apple blossoms are just about to burst open. I'll pick you a bunch of violets tomorrow to put on your bookcase. I stood there and watched the stars come out. If you hadn't been measly I'd have come and got you, they were so beautiful."

"I've seen stars before," I said shortly.

"It's a funny thing about problems and being sick and everything," John said. "When you're in the middle of it, it seems so enormous, it seems the only thing in the world. But when you think of the relativity of size it doesn't seem to matter, after all."

"Having measles matters to me even if it doesn't seem to matter to anyone else," I said stuffily. "Anyhow, what do you mean by the relativity of size?"

John went to the east window and pushed aside the curtains. Our house is a hundred miles outside the city, so there are few lights to dim the stars. "Look at that star up there. Bright and beautiful, but it's only a pinprick in the sky. If it has planets we can't see them. And then look at our own solar system."

"You look at it," I said, irritated.

John continued, undaunted. "We're on part of it right now. The earth. Just a small sphere, one of—how many planets is it? I forget."

We'd had it in school the year before, Mercury, Venus, Earth, Mars, Jupiter, planetoids, Saturn, oh—what comes next, is it Pluto? I stuck my face in the pillow and mumbled, "I couldn't care less."

"Just one of maybe a dozen planets of assorted size circling about a larger ball that's our sun," John said. "And then think of the atoms that go to make everything up. That go to make *us* up."

"You think—" I started.

But John said quickly, "Shut up, Vicky, and listen. Do you realize that your body is made up of millions of atoms, and each one is a tiny solar system? And maybe some of these solar systems are like the larger one we live on. Maybe some of them have inhabited planets with flourishing civilizations. It's all a question of the relativity of size. We really don't know anything about size except that we don't understand it at all."

I shivered. I was hot with fever but I shivered anyhow. "Shut up. You make me feel as though I'm mostly thin air, when I think about being made out of atoms. And now to be made of inhabited planets—of all the idiotic notions, John Austin. What does that make me, a galaxy? Galaxy Austin, that's me."

"Well," John said, "Mother said I was just to give you the ginger ale and see if I could help make you more comfortable for the night. She or Daddy'll look in on you later. Here, I'll straighten out your bed, you've got it all messed up." He pulled the bottom sheet from both sides till it was taut under me—my bed's an odd size that doesn't take fitted sheets—and turned over my pillow, and it felt better. Then he said good night and left me, not a bit cross at me because of my bad temper, as I'd been at him the night he had flu.

But that's what I mean about John. Things like that. Like

talking to me about stars and the relativity of size and stuff. The other kids, the ones we go to school with, don't talk like that. It's not that John does it often, but he does it. It's partly, I suppose, because Mother and Daddy discuss things at the dinner table. And then Daddy belongs to a group of doctors that get together once a month to discuss things, not medicine, but philosophy and economics and stuff like that, and Daddy has been letting John sit and listen in when the meetings are at our house. But what I mean is, we're used to John. Until you get to really know John he can be difficult, but he's handsome and bright and infuriating and peculiar and our brother and we take him for granted.

But he isn't like anybody else's brother, and the other kids don't see him the way we do. One thing that has been a big help to him is having Dave Ulrich for a friend. Dave is a head shorter than John, but he's built like a bull; he's nearly two years older than John, but they're in the same grade, and it sort of makes John seem more okay to be seen with Dave. He and Dave don't discuss things; Dave's not a talker. They *do* things together. When they were little they started to dig a hole that would go all the way down to China. They dug in Dave's back yard and they got down ten feet before Mr. Ulrich decided it was dangerous and ordered them to quit.

Then they built the tree house in our big maple, and they took a couple of old bikes and two old lawn mowers they bought for ten dollars and made a car that would run. Dave isn't very smart at school. I don't mean he's dumb or anything; his I.Q.'s probably fine. He just doesn't care about books unless he's looking something up about how to build one of his machines. This means he's okay in anything that's mathematical, but he'd probably flunk everything else if John didn't push him through. Dave's father has a big lumber business, and Dave's going to go in with him as soon as he gets out of high school, though I know Mrs. Ulrich wishes he'd study enough to go to college.

Schoolwork's always been easy for John. Lots of kids hide their report cards because they aren't very good, but John doesn't want people to see his because they're too good. He says it's bad enough being so nearsighted he can't see the blackboard without his glasses, so he's already pegged as being an egghead.

Suzy and I get good report cards, too, but not as good as John's. I'm good at English and spoken reports and history, but I have a terrible struggle with math. Suzy's memory will pull her through almost anything, and she says she has to get in the habit of getting reasonable report cards if she wants to get into medical school—and she does. Suzy and John have always known what they want to do when they're grown up; John wants to go into space in some way or other, and he's already reading a lot of astrophysics. And Suzy's wanted to be a doctor ever since she could talk. As for me—what? I wish I knew.

Mother and Daddy shake their heads about Rob; he has a big vocabulary; he plunges into words the way other people plunge into water, and no topic is too big or grownup for him to discuss, from war to sex to pollution, but he's just learned to recognize the alphabet and he's not in the least interested in learning to read, and all the rest of us could read when we were five.

Maggy's report cards are up and down. She'd been to private schools before she came to live with us, and she's ahead of her grade in some things, and behind in others. As to what she wants to do when she's grown up, she'd better marry a millionaire who can give her everything she wants.

But to get back to John. Of course the Sunday after I got measles I was still in bed, though I was beginning to feel lots better. I was still covered with a rash and looked repulsive, but I did feel like playing a game of darts with John, and light didn't bother my eyes any more, so I was working through a pile of books. I played and played Mother's records, and laughed at the funny ones and cried at the sad ones. And Saturday evening I got out of bed and went downstairs to watch a Cousteau TV special on endangered species.

Sunday morning, Mother made waffles for breakfast, and Suzy brought me up a tray with waffles and maple syrup and a cup of cocoa with a big blob of whipped cream on it, and it tasted marvelous, the first time anything had tasted really good since I had measles.

Then everybody started off for Sunday school and church and I curled up and took a little nap, and then pushed up my pillows and took a book from my pile and began to read. I was alone in the house but I had all the animals with me, so I wasn't lonely. Rochester lay on the floor by my bed, and Colette was on the foot of the bed, at my feet; Prunewhip, the splotchy colored cat, came pat-patting upstairs and jumped on the bed, too, and sat on my chest and began purring loudly and then kneading her front claws into my neck. I kept shoving her paws away, or trying to push her claws back into their soft sheaths, but she was determined to enjoy herself in her own way, so I had to pull the blanket up over my neck and leave her to it.

I was deep in my book when I heard the kitchen door open and shut. I looked at my little clock that Grandfather gave me for Christmas, and it wasn't time for anybody to be home from church yet; I wondered who on earth it could be. Then I heard rather stealthy footsteps coming up the back stairs and I called out, "Who is it?"

Maggy's voice called back, "It's us," and I wondered what kind of trouble she'd got into now, and then she and John appeared in the doorway.

What a sight!

Maggy's black hair was wild, as though it hadn't been combed or brushed for several years, and her good Sunday dress was ripped, the skirt half pulled off the waist, and had a big, jagged tear in one sleeve. And John! One of John's eyes was all swollen and puffy and there was a cut across his eyebrow and he didn't have on his glasses, and without his glasses John is half blind. His nose had been bleeding, too, and his collar was bloody and torn. It was obvious that Maggy had been crying, and I couldn't tell whether or not John had. I practically jumped out of bed, I was so startled. Colette started to bark, the high yelp she gives when she's upset. Prunewhip jumped down off the bed and swished out of the room. Rochester got up and went and stood by John and Maggy and growled, low and deep in his throat, as though to dare anybody to come near them when he was around.

John petted him, saying, "Oh, Rochester, I wish you'd been over in the churchyard half an hour ago."

"But what on earth happened?" I demanded.

John gave a very lopsided grin. "We were in a fight."

"Who? Why? Do Mother and Daddy know? Where are the others?"

"Hold it," John said. "We'd better go wash before we do anything else."

"No you don't!" I cried. "You tell me what happened first!"

John gave Maggy a funny kind of rough hug. John has never been one for hugging and kissing, so this was all the more remarkable.

"I got involved in a monstrous battle," John said, "and Maggy was coming down from the Sunday-school room and saw me, and she lit into the boys like a hurricane and did her best to rescue me. It was a doggone good best, too. If it hadn't been for Maggy I'd have had a sight worse licking than I got."

"But why were you getting a licking?" I asked. "Where was Dave?" I didn't think anybody'd dare pick a fight with John if Dave was around.

John gave that funny, lopsided grin again and I realized that his lip was cut and swollen, too. "Dave has measles. Come on, Mag, let's wash up."

"No!" I shouted. "Tell me what happened."

"I think I'd better sit down," John said. "I feel wuzzy." He flopped onto the rocker and closed his eyes, and his eyes without glasses were as strange-looking as the cuts and bruises on the rest of his face.

"Where are your glasses?" I asked.

"Smashed. You all right, Maggy?"

"No," Maggy said. "I'm mad. John was fighting all by him-

146

self, with at least a dozen boys on top of him. It wasn't fair. And I didn't have a chance to run up to the Sunday-school room to get Suzy or Rob to help. It wasn't fair. It was the meanest thing I ever saw."

"But what happened?" I asked again.

"Okay," John said. "Let's make it brief, Mag. Mr. Jenkins wasn't there. Nanny and Izzy said there was something wrong with the big deep freeze in their store. He came hurrying after the big battle was over, but that was too late to do me any good."

"What does Mr. Jenkins have to do with it, anyhow?"

"Well, he is the Sunday school superintendant after all, and he always does the opening service for the Sunday school," John said. "You know that. Added to which, Mr. Vining's away this week."

Mr. Vining's the minister. This explained nothing. "What's all this got to do with you?"

"When it was obvious Mr. Jenkins wasn't going to get to church on time, Mr. Ulrich asked me to do it," John said.

"To do what?"

John gave a funny sort of groan. "The opening service."

"It wasn't fair," Maggy protested again. "I heard Aunt Victoria telling Uncle Wallace Mr. Ulrich should never have asked it of John."

Mr. Ulrich teaches the high-school Sunday-school class, and I guess he's sort of second in charge if Mr. Vining isn't there, because sometimes he gives the opening service.

"But he asked me," John said. "He kind of looked around the church. He looked us all over, and his eye lit on me, and he said, 'I'm willing to bet John Austin can get up there and do the opening service for us. How about it, John?' What was I to do? There was nothing I wanted to do less, but I felt I was sort of stuck with it; if I didn't do it I'd be letting Mr. Ulrich down— and Dave, too. At first I didn't say anything, and then Mr. Ulrich said, 'How about it, John?' and I said, 'Okay, Mr. Ulrich, I'll try.' And I had to get up and go to the front of the church and everybody was watching me and some of the boys were grinning, and I thought, I'll show them. So I gave the call to worship, and then had everybody sing *Holy, Holy, Holy*, to give myself time to think. Then I told one of Grandfather's stories, the one about the shoemaker who was so poor and yet he helped all those people—you know the one, it goes with the part in the Bible about if you do it unto the least of these you do it unto me."

"It was a wonderful story," Maggy said. "The girls all thought you were marvelous."

"Yes," John said, "that was the trouble. And I made one terrific goof."

"What?" I asked.

"I took off my glasses."

"But why! You know you can't see two feet in front of your nose without them."

"That's exactly why," John said. "I thought if I couldn't see the kids I wouldn't be so scared. I was afraid if somebody made a face at me or giggled or looked as though they thought I was a dope or something, I'd forget what I was saying and not be able to go through with it. So I took off my glasses so everybody'd look like a vague blur and I couldn't see who was who, or what they were thinking, or anything. But a lot of them thought I was doing it to show off."

"But you weren't——"

"Of course I wasn't. But they thought I was."

"It was those dopey girls," Maggy explained, "giggling and carrying on and saying how dreamy he looked without his glasses."

"I don't think anybody listened to a word I said." John sighed, heavily. "That's almost the worst of it. Maybe some of the little kids listened to the story, but nobody else. Well, then we had the collection, and I had two of the smallest kids take it. Maybe that was being a coward, but I felt safer that way. And then I had to do the prayer."

"What did you say?" I asked. "Did you make it up?"

"No, I was too scared. I said the St. Francis Prayer." And he began to say it softly, as though he needed it for himself. "Lord, make me an instrument of your peace. Where there is hatred, let me sow love; where there is injury, pardon; where there is doubt, faith; where there is discord, union; where there is despair, hope; where there is darkness, light; and where there is sadness, joy. O divine master, grant that I may not so much seek to be consoled as to console; to be understood as to understand; to be loved as to love; for it is in giving that we receive; it is in pardoning that we are pardoned; and it is in dying that we are born to eternal life." He took a deep breath. "Well, then we went to our classes. But I knew trouble was coming. A couple of the kids kind of poked me and whispered things like, 'You just think you're the most beautiful boy, don't you?' And Mr. Ulrich made it worse by trying to set me up as an example to the rest of the class and I couldn't shut him up. If Dave had been there *he'd* have shut his father up. When classes were over, the Sunday-school teachers were supposed to be meeting about something, and the minute I got outdoors the kids were waiting for me, and one of them said, 'Got your glasses on now, haven't you, gorgeous?' and I said, 'Yeah, what's it to you,' and he said, 'Take 'em off so we can see those dreamy eyes,' and I said, 'Take 'em off yourself,' and that's how it started."

"They were cowards," Maggy said, "all of them together and John all alone, and when his glasses got busted they knew he couldn't even see what he was doing. But he was doing okay. I came out in the middle of it, 'cause someone told me what was going on, and I was just so mad I jumped on Sammy Calahan's back and pulled his hair and then I saw somebody else's leg sticking out and I bit that. I don't know whose it was, but I bet I drew blood."

"Kind of backhanded tactics," John said, "but they surely helped. The others weren't fighting exactly fair, either."

"What about Mother and Daddy?" I asked. "Do they know about it?"

"Dad brought us home," John said.

"Did he break it up?"

"No. One of the girls ran in and got the teachers out of their meeting and they all came out and everybody kind of got off me and Maggy was fighting so hard by then she didn't even realize the fight was over till Mr. Ulrich pulled her off one of the boys. Then people started coming to church, and Mother and Daddy came up the path and saw us, and Dad brought us home, and that's all."

Maggy gave a contented sort of sigh. "Maybe Suzy and Rob don't even know about it yet. They were in the upstairs Sunday-school room."

"Somebody's told them by now," I said.

John stood up. "Well, I guess I better grope my way to the bathtub. I'll take the upstairs bathroom, it's colder, and you can use the one downstairs, Mag."

Maggy ran off, and I thought she seemed different than she had been with us. Mostly she's pulled against us, tried to be different, to have special privileges, to be a TV star, and suddenly she seemed not only more like one of us but as though she actually finally wanted to be one of us. And once again I was glad she hadn't been thrown to the lions.

John said, "Well, see you later, Vic," and went off with Rochester thumping anxiously at his heels. I heard him bump into a chair or something, and then a moment later I heard his bathwater running. I lay in bed, stroking Colette's ear and thinking about what had happened, till John came back in, wrapped in his bath towel, and sat down in the Boston rocker again.

"I get on okay with Dave," he said. "I thought I got on okay with the others, too."

I wasn't sure what to say. I murmured, "Oh, John . . ." and if I'd been Mother I could have gone to him and put my arms around him and given him some love. But I was only his kid sister, Vicky, and all I could do was lie there and look at him, his body firm and lean and still white from winter, his face all battered up, and the cut by his eye going right through one of his eyebrows. Without his glasses his eyes seemed much bigger than usual, and they looked unhappy. His reddy-brown hair was wet, and he'd slicked it down, but a tuft of it stuck up in the back.

"Well," I said at last, "maybe it comes down to muffins again." (About muffins I will explain in just a minute.)

John nodded. "Sometimes being muffiny can be very tempting. Listen, Vicky, as soon as you're better let's have a meeting. Is it okay if I propose Maggy? As far as I'm concerned, she qualified this morning."

I remembered Maggy's look as she'd gone down the hall to take her bath, so I said, "It's okay with me if you think it'll be okay with the others."

"We've never turned down anybody anyone's put up, yet."

"It's never been anybody who didn't belong here," I said, "and Maggy's really only a visitor."

"That's a muffiny remark if there ever was one," John said.

I thought it over for a moment. "Yes, I guess it was."

"Do I look awful?" he asked.

"Kind of like a prize-fighter."

"That's one thing I'm not and never will be. Well, I'd better go get some clothes on."

He'd just gone out the door when the phone rang and he headed into Mother and Daddy's room, bumping into things on the way.

I heard him say, "Dave! . . . But you have measles! . . . Well, it wasn't your father's fault . . . No, if I'd done it differently, or something . . . well, sure I'm not mad at him . . . They home from church already? . . . Well, sure, I'm mad at the others. I was so mad by the time they broke it up I was be-

152

ginning to enjoy the fight . . . Listen, you'd better get back to bed. You don't want any secondary infections . . . Sure. Be over to see you as soon as you're feeling better. Hey, Dave, I sure look a beaut, you ought to see me . . . Okay. Bye."

As he hung up I heard the door downstairs open, and Colette leaped off my bed and dashed down, barking her welcoming bark; and then there was the sound of a small herd of elephants and Suzy and Rob came dashing up the stairs. And then Mother and Daddy came along and then the telephone rang again, and it was the father of one of the kids in the fight, to complain about John's starting it! And the rest of the day was like that, a peaceful Sunday, all full of sound and fury.

Mr. Ulrich called, very upset, and Mother had to reassure him that John wasn't seriously hurt, and he really wasn't to blame, it was just one of those things. The father of another of the boys called up in a rage because John had given his boy a bloody nose, and Daddy told him off about that.

In between times Daddy cleaned up John's face and put a bandage over the cut above his eye, and told him not to read till his glasses were fixed. Maggy had a big scratch on one leg, but otherwise it was her clothes that got it; she was okay. And Mr. Jenkins called up, all worried, and Daddy had to calm him down. "Look, boys will be boys, and problems like this happen occasionally. Nobody was badly hurt, and maybe they've all learned a lesson. But let's not have the whole village get into a turmoil over it." All in all, we had about as much Sunday peace and quiet as we'd have had at a three-ring circus. Mr. Jenkins came over with a big carton of ice cream from his store as a peace offering.

The next day one of the Granby boys got into real trouble. He "borrowed" one of the Hendricks' horses and the horse stepped into a hole and sprained its foot, and he was scared to tell the Hendricks he'd taken the horse and what had happened, but of course he didn't get away with it, and in the ensuing excitement John and the Sunday-school fight got forgotten. John got new glasses and his face unswelled and his cuts healed and things went back to normal.

A week later I went back to school, and so did Dave, and suddenly we were plunged into summer. It had been a long, cold, snowy, rainy spring. In fact, there was hardly any real spring to speak of at all, and then all at once at the end of May it was summer, with hot, sunny days and swimming in the pond after school, and we all went to sleep lying on top of our beds with the covers pulled down, and Mother and Daddy pulled our sheets up when they came upstairs at night.

On Friday at breakfast John asked if we could have a picnic up Hawk Mountain that night.

"Why, John? I don't see why not, but is it for anything special?"

"Yes," he said. "Muffins. We want to take in a new member."

"I see. Okay with the others?"

"The picnic or the member?"

"Both."

"The picnic's fine. I haven't brought the member up yet."

Maggy was putting her cereal dish in the sink, something it took her months to remember to do. Mother glanced at her. "Am I right in my guess as to the new member?"

John grinned. "Could be."

"All right, John. Just don't make it too late for the little ones, will you? What do you want to take for supper?"

"Could you make us a big dish of baked beans with hot dogs cut up in it? You know the kind. If we start out with it good and hot it'll be okay. I thought I'd ask Dave and Betsey Ulrich to bring a salad, and Izzy and Nanny Jenkins can bring ice cream and Coke." Izzy is Nanny's older sister and a good friend of John's.

"All right," Mother said. "I'll drive you up at five and come for you at nine. Okay?"

"Thanks," John said. "That'll be super."

So at five we got in the car, the four of us and Maggy, and picked up Dave and Betsey, and Izzy and Nanny, and Pedro Xifra. John didn't ask Pedro to bring anything, because his parents don't have much money and aren't likely to. Mr. Xifra's a tenant farmer, and he stays on Creighton's farm and works long hard hours, with little time for his family. Pedro helps out as much as he can when he gets home from school and weekends. We knew he'd worked extra hard to be ready when we came for him.

First we stopped off for Dave and Betsey. Dave had a big wooden bowl with tomatoes and celery and Betsey a tea towel wrapped around lettuce and a big jar of dressing to pour over it. Luckily, at the last minute Mother'd remembered we'd need something to eat our food with, and off, so we had a stack of paper plates and cups and forks as well as our hot dish of beans. I think Mr. Ulrich still feels kind of bad about John, because just as we were about to leave he came up from his lumber yard in Clovenford and handed us a big box of cookies. Then we went to get the Jenkinses. Mr. Jenkins put a big case of soda in the back of our station wagon, and Izzy and Nanny had ice cream packed in dry ice.

Then we went to get Pedro. He's in the middle of a whole lot of kids. Their house is across the road from the barns, and needs painting, and last summer their stoop started to fall off, and it would have fallen off if Pedro hadn't fixed it.

He was waiting for us by the mailbox. He had a brown paper bag with him and he said he'd made egg-salad sandwiches. John said, "Oh, great, Pedro." The eggs must have come from Pedro's own chickens.

Mother drove the station wagon, which was by now pretty jammed, up the dirt road to the top of Hawk, and we all tumbled out, carrying the picnic stuff. Mother waved and honked and took off, and John and Izzy got the picnic all organized, and we ate and talked and laughed and the evening was warm, but not hot, with a breeze cool enough so that we put on our sweaters or jackets.

When we'd cleaned everything up and put all the trash in the big trash can, John said, "You've probably all guessed what we're here for."

"It looks like a meeting of the anti-muffin club," Pedro said.

"How'd you guess? And I wanted a meeting because I'm proposing a new member."

He was smiling, and I looked over at Maggy and she was sitting looking a little pink and flustered.

Pedro said, "If it's Maggy, I'm all for it," and smiled at her.

Nanny said, "It must be Maggy, because all the rest of us are members."

John said to Pedro, "We had a whopperoozo of a fight in the churchyard, and Maggy pitched in to help me, and didn't give a hoot what anybody thought."

Pedro wasn't around at the fight, because his family goes to St. Francis Church in Clovenford.

Izzy asked, "Does she know about muffins? Do you, Maggy?"

Maggy said, "I like them when Aunt Victoria makes them for breakfast," and everybody laughed, even Rob. One thing Rob's learned is that he couldn't belong, being so much younger than the rest of us, if he made any noise or disturbance, and he was so thrilled at being included in something that had so many big kids in it, that he sat quiet as a little mouse at all the meetings, with an expression so solemn it was funny. The main reason we let Rob be in the club was that it was a family thing, and then it got expanded, and if ever anybody was perfect antimuffin material, it's Rob. Added to which, he really kind of started the club.

"We'd better tell her about muffins, then," Nanny said. "That is, if she's really interested."

"I'm not exactly hungry right now." Maggy patted her stomach. "But I'm fascinated." Her black hair was pushed back from her ears and it fell softly down to her shoulders. Her face looked white against it and her eyes were dark. Even though she had on jeans and an old red sweater that had once been mine, I thought that in comparison with the rest of us she looked very much a city person.

There was a pause while everybody waited for somebody

else to speak. Betsey said, "John or one of the Austins ought to tell her about it, because they started it."

"Well," John said, "Rob really started it. It was about a year ago, and Uncle Douglas was up for the weekend."

John continued, "He came up without a girlfriend, but the weekend before, he came up *with* a girlfriend."

"Does he always bring his girlfriends up?" Maggy asked.

"Usually. We kind of look them over. Some of them we like and some of them we don't like, and we didn't like this one."

"Sort of like Sally?" Maggy asked.

"Even worse, if you can believe it, and younger. She kept asking questions about the family, Mother's and Daddy's families," I said, "wanting to know all about forebears and stuff."

John started laughing. "Remember the aunt's sisters?"

I laughed, too. It was really hilarious. This girl kept talking about her ancestors, and Rob went to Mother and said, "Her aunt must have had an awful lot of sisters."

So John told about that and we all laughed, the way you laugh an extra lot on a picnic when you've filled up with good food and are feeling warm and happy.

Maggy said, "I still don't know about muffins."

So John explained. What happened was that Uncle Douglas came back the next weekend and told us that he and the girlfriend were through. And then he gave us a sort of lecture, about how we shouldn't worry about families and the right ethnic background (I looked at Pedro as John was explaining), but you should like them or dislike them for themselves. And Uncle Douglas went on to say that his ex-girlfriend thought that where people were born made them what they are.

Well, that same afternoon, about a year ago, Prunewhip had kittens. We knew she was going to have kittens, and we ran down to the cellar to her bed, but she wasn't there, and we looked in the garage and Daddy's office and under all the beds and in the closets and everywhere we could think of, but we couldn't find her. Then, when Mother went to turn on the oven for the muffins she was making, she noticed that the oven door was partway open, and she opened it all the way, and there was Prunewhip with five kittens! We'd had kittens all over the place, but never in the oven before, and Prunewhip looked very pleased with herself, and Mother said, ah, well, we'd do without the oven that evening.

And John said, a bit sarcastically, "Uncle Douglas, would your ex-girlfriend think the kittens were muffins because they were born in the oven?" Rob thought that was awfully funny and when he stopped laughing he started chanting.

> *"Kittens are muffins*
> *In ovens and puffins."*

Suzy interrupted and said, "They'd all have to be exactly alike, each one just like the other, instead of all different like Prunewhip's kittens."

John said, suddenly serious, "I'd hate that. But that's what a lot of people want—everybody the same like a row of muffins."

So that's how the muffin club got started. Maggy said, "Go on, tell me more."

"Well, that's really it," John said. "You can see how we went on from the kittens not being muffins because they were born in the oven, to starting the anti-muffin club. Uncle Douglas says it will help us avoid the dangers of conformity."

Izzy lay on her back, looking up at the deepening sky. "Your Uncle Douglas is very nice, but most of the time I don't know what he's talking about."

"All he means is that you shouldn't be afraid to be yourself, even if it means being different."

"Like lots of grownups," Betsey said. "Most of them. Always so worried about what somebody's going to think."

"So do you want to belong?" Suzy asked.

Funnily enough, Maggy got all flustered. "I'd love to, if you really want me."

"We wouldn't have called the meeting if we didn't," Suzy said. "We thought maybe you'd think it was silly."

"Why?" Maggy sounded indignant.

Nanny said, "Just that it's something you've probably never had to think about before, with the way you lived before you came to stay with the Austins."

Maggy asked stiffly, "What do you mean?"

John said quickly, "Well, you've never been much around muffiny people. Your grandfather's certainly not a muffin, the way he didn't take Sally seriously when she told him how awful we were."

"We were pretty awful," I said.

"Yes, but not the way Sally thought. And your parents don't sound as though they were much like most people, your father being a test pilot, for instance. And Aunt Elena's certainly not a muffin. She goes around giving concerts and practices at least five hours a day and it certainly doesn't bother her that she isn't like anybody else."

"Is Uncle Douglas an anti-muffin?" Maggy asked.

"Well, sure."

"And Aunt Victoria and Uncle Wallace? Do they belong to the club?"

"They're certainly anti-muffins," I said, "but they don't belong to the club."

"Why not?"

"If you start putting parents in, it can get complicated," John said. "Sometimes there are parents who are muffins and children who aren't, and vice versa." Nobody said anything. It was a little ticklish. We're terribly fond of the Ulrichs, but they're really kind of muffiny. Mr. Jenkins certainly isn't a muffin, practicing his cello in the back room of the store when there aren't many customers, but Mrs. Jenkins is; she's always worrying about what the neighbors will think, and since they run the store and are always in the public eye, the neighbors know a good deal about them. The Xifras aren't muffins, but then, on the other hand, they aren't anti-muffins either, except Pedro, and I think Mrs. Xifra'd really love to be a muffin.

"Could I ask another question?" Maggy asked.

"Sure."

"What's the point to this club?"

"There isn't any particular point," John said. "Just to help us not act like muffins, I guess. If you know there are other people who feel the same way you do, then it gives you courage to stand up for your principles. You were acting anti-muffiny when you ploughed into all those kids after Sunday school. You weren't worried about what they were going to think of you, or if you were going to be hurt, or if it was going to make you unpopular."

"Oh," Maggy said. "Like that new girl who came into our grade last week. She comes from Tennessee and she has a funny accent and everybody teases her. You mean if I go up to her on Monday and try to be nice to her, and see what she's really like, and don't care what the others think of me for doing it, that'll be anti-muffin."

"Good," Pedro approved. "That's it, Maggy. I used to have an accent, too, when I started school. John and Dave kept my life from being hell."

"And it's partly just for fun," John said. "The club, I mean. We don't have any officers or dues or special times for meetings or anything. It's just a time people who like each other can get together and have a good time, the way we're doing this evening."

"Let's sing," Izzy suggested. "Nanny'll sing us a solo."

Nanny was lying on her back chewing a fresh new blade of grass. "I might surprise you someday," she said lazily. Actually, her voice isn't that bad.

Izzy started singing the *Ash Grove*. We all love the Welsh melody, and we sing it to words Mr. Jenkins taught us, and it's kind of the anti-muffin song.

> *"His law he enforces,*
> *the stars in their courses,*
> *the sun in his orbit*
> *obediently shine."*

Izzy sang, and we all joined in.

> *"The hills and the mountains,*
> *The rivers and fountains,*
> *The deeps of the ocean*
> *Proclaim God Divine.*
>
> *We, too, should be voicing*
> *Our love and rejoicing*
> *With glad adoration*
> *A song let us raise,*
>
> *Till all things now living*
> *Unite in thanksgiving,*
> *To God in the highest,*
> *Hosanna and praise!"*

Izzy's clear, pure soprano was like a flute. Rob got up from where he was sitting and plunked himself down in front of Izzy and put his head in her lap. Izzy started ruffling his soft, light brown hair, and kept on singing, and Rob closed his eyes and I knew that in a few minutes he would be asleep. Then Izzy started the *Tallis Canon*. We all know the parts to that, so we joined in. John was singing bass, and I suddenly realized how deep his voice was, and it seemed hardly any time since it had been high and clear like Rob's. Izzy was looking at him, and her eyes were like Colette's when she looks at Daddy when he's sitting in the red leather chair and she hopes he's going to give her a tidbit. And suddenly I realized that John was growing up, and Izzy and Betsey were beginning to wear makeup as a matter of course. We were all growing up and everything was going to change; it would never be the same again. I felt absolutely desolate with sadness, and suddenly I jumped up, shouting, "Let's play something silly, let's play touch tag," and the next minute we were all running around wildly, and John and Izzy and Nanny and Pedro and Dave just as laughing and panting as the rest of us, and I felt a little better. We ran and shouted till it got dark, and then we sat down again and watched the stars come out and Pedro told us about them, the names of the different constellations, and how far away the stars are, and how big.

"We were going with Mother and Daddy to study the stars, the night——" Suzy stopped herself, and I knew she had been going to say, "the night Uncle Hal was killed."

"What night?" Maggy asked.

We hadn't gone, and the autumn had slipped away and winter had come and we hadn't gone.

"What night?" Maggy asked again.

"One night last autumn," John said, "before you came. Is that Vega of the Lyre, Pedro?"

Mother had taken John and me to Hawk, but that was different, a part of grief.

Pedro pointed out Vega for John, and then he said, "I love stars. I'm going to learn everything I can about them. I love them better than anything in the world. Better even than people or books. I'd give my right arm to work at Palomar or Mount Wilson or someplace like that."

"Maybe you will," I said. I like Pedro a lot. When he decides he wants to learn something, or change in some way, he usually manages to do it.

"Well, I'm going to Regional Trade School," Pedro said, "to learn to be the electrician I've always wanted to be, but stars will be my lifelong hobby. Hey, look, kids, a shooting star! You don't see many in May.

"The thing about stars," Pedro went on, "is that when you're with stars, people don't matter so much, or things like being dirty and untidy and quarreling, and nobody else caring about anything you care about, and things like that."

"We care," Nanny said softly.

And John tried to lighten things by giving me a poke and saying, "It's all a question of the relativity of size."

"I hear a car," Suzy said. "I bet it's Mother."

It was, but she didn't rush us home. Instead, she came and sat with us for a few minutes first, so we didn't have any feeling of being pushed when we finally piled into the station wagon. Rob was so sound asleep that we had to carry him, and he slept in my lap all the way home, and then Daddy came out and carried him up to bed. So of course he was asleep when we said prayers and didn't hear when Maggy said in her God Bless, "And thank you, God, for the best time I ever had."

The Visit to the Stable

Our grandfather, Mother's father, lives in a stable.

Maybe I'd better explain a little about this.

We've never known our Austin grandparents, because Daddy's mother died when Uncle Douglas was born, and Daddy's father, when Daddy was still in school. Grammy Eaton died about five years ago. John and I remember her very well, but I don't think the little ones do. Well, of course, Rob doesn't. Grandfather Eaton is a minister, and while Mother was growing up they moved several times, from one big old parsonage to another. Then, when Grandfather retired, they moved to Seven Bay Island, where they'd always gone for their vacations. They had friends who had a big house there, up on the only hill on the island, and at the peak of the hill (our family seems to like houses on hills, even though it means a lot of wind, particularly in winter) is an old stable. Grammy talked their friends into selling the stable to her and Grandfather about five years before Grandfather retired, and they spent the summers fixing it up and getting it ready to live in all year round.

Grandfather has what Mother says is his only great vice: he cannot pass a bookstore. She says it's like someone who can't pass a bar without going in for a drink. Grandfather cannot pass a bookstore without going in and buying a book. He's not a bibliophile, he's a bibliomaniac. (Look *those* up in your dictionary!) Of course, Mother shouldn't talk. It's like the pot calling the kettle black or people in glass houses throwing stones.

So one thing Grandfather and Grammy always had to think of wherever they went was bookcases for Grandfather's thousands and thousands of books. He couldn't bear to think of any of them lying in packing cases. They all had to be out on shelves, and none behind each other, either, so he could get at them whenever he wanted; and since he's always consulting books for one reason or other, that's often. And if you ask Grandfather for a book, in spite of the fact that there are so many of them, he always knows exactly where and on which shelf it is, and can get it for you without a moment's hesitation. I feel that way about books, too. Most of the time, Mother and Daddy don't even call me "bookworm." They just call me "worm."

So, anyhow, what Grandfather and Grammy did when they bought the stable was to leave up the horses' stalls and build bookcases in them. Is that where the word "stalls" comes from in libraries, I wonder. From horses' stalls? Because Grandfather's stalls look rather like stalls or stacks in a library. They take up so much room that there isn't any real living room, just one double stall, and it has books in it, too, with a sofa and a couple of easy chairs and a table and a lamp. Grandfather has his desk in one of the stalls. And in one of them there's nothing but children's books, especially for us and the other grandchildren, but none of us see very much of them, the other grandchildren, I mean, because when Aunt Sue married she went out to California to live, and they don't get East very often.

If there's anything we love it's to go visit Grandfather in the stable.

Every once in a while Mother says that Daddy will have to have a vacation or he won't be able to go on, and one of those times came that June, just as school was almost over. It was the first big thunderstorm of the year. Daddy was home early that day, and Mother was saying, "Wally, you've been driving yourself unmercifully. You simply have to have a few days off."

Daddy said, "Look out the window," and we looked out the big kitchen windows and watched the storm roll across the hills, great drenching sheets of rain, almost a cloudburst, and enormous sky-splitting flashes of lightning and crashes of thunder. We all sat there together watching it, and it was beautiful and I wasn't a bit scared, but I would have been if I'd been alone. I remember one big thunderstorm came the day of Rob's second birthday. He'd been given a flashlight at his birthday party, and every time a flash of lightning came he clapped his hands gleefully and yelled out, "Flashlight!"

Anyhow, to get back to the particular storm, after an enormous flash and crash that made us all jump it was so close Daddy said, "School's over next week, and I don't have any maternity cases due for the rest of this month. I'll try to arrange it so we can all get away, and drive up to your father's."

Maggy had never been to Grandfather's, but we told her all about it, and she was as excited as the rest of us in no time, though at first she acted kind of funny about going to visit anyone who lived in a stable.

By the time we were through dinner that night the storm was over and the rain had stopped. When we went up to bed it was quiet and still, and we were all excited and happy at the idea of going in just about ten days to the island to visit Grandfather.

Mother read to us, an exciting story in one of her old *Chatterboxes*, and just as we were about to start prayers Rob asked, "Mother, who was the first man?"

"I don't know, darling; nobody knows. We call him Adam, but nobody really knows."

"But somebody must know."

"Nobody knows, Rob, except God."

"Well, Mother, it's very peculiar, because if somebody, if Adam, came first, wouldn't he have had to have a mother and father?"

Mother laughed and said, "It's a good thing we're going to visit Grandfather so soon. You can ask him, Rob. Explaining theology and evolution to a very small boy is too big an order for me."

While we were in bed, the west wind sprang up and blew all night with all its might and main. It blew so hard it woke me up. Our house braced itself on its hill and stood firm, but quivering. As the wind drove itself against the garage and the office and the side of the house, it was as though a giant hand were taking hold of my bed and shaking it. I was very glad that the night-light was on in the bathroom, that Rob was asleep in the little bed, and that Mother and Daddy were right across the hall.

But in the morning, after the thunderstorm of the day before and the windstorm of the night, we awoke to a warm, soft sunshine and a feeling of early summer in the air, the first real feeling we'd had that summer was here. After breakfast, till time to walk down the hill to the school bus, we ran about the garden, and suddenly the peonies and wild roses were almost ready to burst open. We ran all the way down the hill to the school bus, with Mr. Rochester and Colette dashing ahead and then coming back and running on again, and Prunewhip and Creamy stalking just in front of us, tails erect and proud.

We thought the ten days till time to leave would take forever, particularly because right after Daddy'd said we'd go, things began to be queer. First of all we noticed that Daddy and Mother were talking things over by themselves more than usual, much more than you'd think a simple trip to the island, which we'd taken dozens of times before, could make them do. They kept going into Daddy's office and shutting the door, so we knew something was up. Then that weekend Aunt Elena came up, and it was the first time we'd seen her since the weekend of Sally and the ice storm. And Maggy said she'd heard Mother and Daddy and Aunt Elena talking about her.

"If anybody tries to take me away from here I'll shoot them," she said, quite violently. "It's just awful at Grampa's,

170

always having to whisper and tiptoe so I won't disturb him. I wouldn't mind going to live with Aunt Elena or Uncle Douglas, but I won't go anywhere else. I refuse."

We didn't say that if her grandfather decided he wanted her, she couldn't refuse.

And then Daddy called Uncle Douglas in New York. I found out about that by accident. He was using the phone upstairs in the bedroom, and I picked up the phone downstairs to call Nanny about something, and though I hung right up, I heard Uncle Douglas's voice saying, "It will be much better if you can come down and talk to the lawyers yourself, Wally." I told John this, but it didn't help very much.

Aunt Elena left Sunday evening. Nobody said anything more that we could hear, but we all felt that it must be about Maggy, and we were upset. She still did all kinds of things we didn't like, but, nevertheless, she'd changed an awful lot since she'd been with us and we'd begun to think of her as part of the family. And you can dislike things about one of your family, but you care about her, too. And she certainly wasn't a muffin.

Well, Mother and Daddy still kept going off into Daddy's office or up to their room, with the door closed—and we are not a family for closing doors—and we still didn't have any more idea for sure what was going on, and John said to me, "Suppose we're all wrong, the way we were about Sally being one of Uncle Douglas's girlfriends, and it isn't Maggy at all?"

"But what else could it be? Mother looks worried about something, and I can't think of anything else that would be worrying her."

"Well, she'd be worried if she and Daddy were going to get

a divorce or something." Then, at his own wild idea, he went pale. "Oh, Vic, you don't suppose that could be it, do you?"

Such a horrible idea had never crossed my mind. I turned on him in fury. "John Austin, don't you ever dare say such a stupid thing again!"

"Well," he said, "I think it's an awful idea, too, but things like that have happened to people. Look at Dave." Dave's parents are divorced.

"But Mother and Daddy love each other!" I shouted. "It's obvious they love each other!"

"Well," John said, "Dave thought his parents loved each other, and Mother and Daddy've been awfully funny lately. Maybe Daddy's met some awful woman and fallen madly in love and is asking for a divorce. That would explain talking to lawyers."

"Or it could be Mother and a heel."

John shook his head. "If Mother'd met anybody we'd know it. It's different with Daddy. Women patients are always supposed to fall in love with their doctor."

I got angry again. "I think you're the most horrible person I've ever known. Daddy kisses Mother when he comes home the way he always does. He wouldn't do that if anything were wrong."

"It might be just a front."

"With Mother?" I asked scornfully. "You know we always know how Mother feels." I stamped off. But John had put the idea into my head, and every few minutes it came sneaking back. I knew it was stupid and untrue, and because John was upset over what had happened to Dave's parents, but I kept looking at it, just to make sure it was still impossible, sort of the way you sometimes keep pressing a bruise to see if it still hurts.

That night, after we'd all turned out our lights and Mother and Daddy were downstairs, John came tiptoeing into Rob's and my room, peered down at Rob to make sure he was sound asleep, and then sat by me on the bed. "Listen, Vic," he said, "I was nuts this afternoon."

"Yes," I said, "I know. But I wish you hadn't thought of it. It bothers me even though I know it couldn't possibly be true."

"Well, it was Dave put it into my mind. But now I know it not only sounds idiotic, it *is* idiotic. I thought of what you said, and when Daddy came home I watched very carefully the way he kissed Mother. He wasn't putting on. Well, good night, Vic." And off he went.

But for the next few days I wanted to shake John for having brought it up.

And then one night after the little ones were in bed and Mother and Daddy and John and I were sitting around the fire, Daddy said, "I guess you two kids have realized Mother and I have been worried about something."

"Not just us two," John said. "The little ones, too. Maggy thinks it's something to do with her. Is it?"

"Yes," Daddy said. "But I'm sorry she's aware of it. The less she has to worry till things are settled one way or other, the better. Can I trust you two not to talk about it?"

"Of course, Daddy," we said.

"The lawyers want Mr. Ten Eyck to make some kind of

decision as to Maggy's future, and he himself realizes that it's bad for her to be living with a constant sense of uncertainty. As long as she feels that this is not her real home, that she's only on a visit, no matter how long a visit, it makes it impossible for her to adjust completely."

"Although she's improved a great deal," Mother said.

"She sure has," John said. "No more shrieks in the middle of the night."

"And she doesn't break our things half as much as she used to."

"Well," Daddy said, "thinking of Maggy, what would you want for her future?"

"I wouldn't want her to go to her grandfather," John said.

"Then what would you want? Vicky?"

"It would be nice if someone could adopt her," I said slowly, "so she could have a real mother and father. It would be lovely if Aunt Elena and Uncle Douglas could get married and adopt her. Then she'd have a mother and father, and if Aunt Elena had to be away, Maggy could be here with us."

"How about it, Dad?" John said.

Mother and Daddy both laughed. "I wonder how Doug and Elena would feel about our rearranging their entire lives for them?" Mother asked.

"Well, if you ask me," John said, "I think the reason none of Uncle Douglas's girlfriends ever pans out is that he's been in love with Aunt Elena for years."

"I think you're right, John," Mother said, "but remember that we must give Aunt Elena time. It's not a year since Uncle Hal's death. She isn't ready to love again quite yet. But she and

Uncle Douglas have always been close, warm friends, and per-haps it's excusable of us to hope that something works out be-tween them."

"If I were a gambler," John said, "I'd lay money on it. How about you, Dad?"

"A conservative amount, at least," Daddy said. "Mean-while, leaving aside the ideal solution you've suggested, what about Maggy?"

"Well, Dad, if you'd asked me a few months ago I'd have said I didn't give a darn about what happened to her as long as you got her out of the house."

"But you do give a darn now?" Mother asked.

"Yes. I do."

"We all do," I said.

"So," Daddy said, "you think maybe we should urge her grandfather to let her stay on with us for, say, another year?"

"Yup."

"Well, I think that's just what we're going to do," Daddy said, "but we're glad you feel about it as we do. Remembering that Maggy isn't an easy child to have about the house, and I don't think she ever will be, even with more security."

"But she's sort of become our responsibility," John said. "We can't just throw her out the way some people do dogs when they come up to the country for the summer and then just let them out of the car somewhere when they're on their way back to the city."

"And a child is more important than a dog, I hope," Mother said, misquoting Alice in the Red Queen's voice.

"So what the plan is, then," Daddy said, "is for us all to go up to the island for a week. I'm going to take that real vacation Mother has been trying to get me to take for so long. And a week on the island with Grandfather sounds mighty good to me, I can tell you. Then, after a week, Mother and I will go down to New York, leaving you children with Grandfather. Mr. Ten Eyck has arranged a meeting for us with the lawyers and Aunt Elena, and we'll also have to go down to the probate court and talk with one of the judges there. Uncle Douglas is going to be at all the meetings, too, which will help, as Mr. Ten Eyck seems to have taken a liking to him. But we have to face the fact that we really haven't the slightest idea what Mr. Ten Eyck's decision will be."

"You mean he might not let her stay with us?" John asked.

"Exactly. He's a very erratic old gentleman. Now, one thing in our favor is that he thought Sally Hough's visit with us was funny, and that he never had any real intention of letting Maggy go to her. But he is seriously considering getting a nurse and governess and keeping the child with him in New York."

"But that would be awful for her!" I exclaimed.

"We think so," Mother said, "but other people may not think our life is as warm and happy and healthy as we think it is. Our biggest hope is Uncle Douglas. Mr. Ten Eyck thinks he is amusing, and he likes his painting, and he's commissioned him to do a painting of Maggy's mother from a series of photographs. Uncle Douglas doesn't like working that way, but he's going to do it for Maggy's sake."

"So that's the story up to now," Daddy said. "Don't say anything to the younger ones about it. It would be a lot harder for Maggy to know her fate is being sealed than for her to have a vague feeling that maybe people are discussing her. And we want the trip to the island to be fun and not spoiled by tensions and anxieties. Okay?"

"Okay," we said.

We had thought it would never be time to leave for the island, or that we mightn't be able to leave at all, because, Maggy's problems aside, with Daddy you never know. But suddenly it was time to pack, and we were going to leave the next morning.

When we got up, all was excitement and sound and fury. Daddy got a call and went tearing down to the hospital, but he promised he'd be back in an hour. Mother made pancakes and sausage for us all so we wouldn't need so much lunch, and she packed a picnic basket for lunch, but I think she had an idea when Daddy went down to the hospital that he wouldn't get back and we wouldn't be able to go. But he did get back, not in an hour, but in an hour and seventeen minutes, which wasn't bad, considering, and Mother gave him a plate of pancakes and sausage and told him to eat them quickly before the phone rang again, and Daddy said not to worry, he wasn't taking any more calls.

Mother told us all to put our bags in the back of the car. We took out the back seat and made the suitcases into a sort of seat and put an old quilt over them, and Suzy and Maggy begged to sit there first, and of course Rob wanted to sit with them, and they didn't want him to, and he cried, and Daddy shouted at us all to go get in the car, he didn't care how we sat as long as he and Mother had the front seat, but we were to get into the car and stay there and be quiet or they'd go without us. We didn't quite believe that, but Daddy sounded as though he half meant it, so we went and got in the car, and Rob finally settled for the middle seat with John and Rochester and me, because Rochester insisted on sitting with Rob and Elephant's Child, though we tried to get him to go in back with Maggy and Suzy, who didn't want him anyhow.

Finally, Mother and Daddy came out to get in the car. Just as we were about to start, Mother said, "Oh, Wally, excuse me, there's something I wanted to do I forgot," and she disappeared into the house again. She was gone a good five minutes and when she came out again she wasn't carrying anything with her or anything, and Daddy said, "What was it you forgot?"

Mother said, "I just painted the seats on both the toilets. There's never any chance to do it. No matter how many signs I put up, you know perfectly well somebody'd forget and sit on the wet paint, so I gave them both a good coat of white paint and they'll be dry by the time we get home."

Daddy laughed and said, "Victoria, you being you, I might have known it would be something like that," and Mother laughed, too, and climbed in beside him, and we were off.

We had gone all the way down the hill to Clovenford, past the hospital, past Daddy's office, past the railroad station, and were starting uphill again at the other side of town when Mother said, "Who's holding Colette?"

Then everybody asked everybody else, and nobody was holding Colette; we'd forgotten her.

Daddy turned the car around and we started for home again. Mother said, "It's one thing forgetting Colette, but do you remember the time Daddy forgot Rob?"

"When did Daddy forget me?" Rob demanded. "How could Daddy forget me?"

"I never heard about that," Maggy said. "Tell me about it, Aunt Victoria."

So Mother told about the time when Rob was just a tiny baby and we were all going, one Sunday afternoon, on a picnic. We each had something to remember, and Daddy was in charge of Rob. He put Rob's car bed in the car, and a bag of diapers, and some Pablum, and I was in charge of the paper plates and cups and napkins and things like that, and John was to watch out for Suzy, and Mother took care of the food, of course, and we all started off, and when we got to the place where we were going to have the picnic, Mother went to get Rob out of the car bed and Daddy had never put him in! He'd left him sound asleep in his crib!

So Mother said forgetting Colette was a mere nothing, and she started us off singing songs. When we got back to the house she was going to go in, but Daddy sent John in after Colette. "If I let you in the house, Vic, you'll find something else that needs a quick coat of paint."

So John came out carrying Colette, and we started off again. What with Daddy's trip to the hospital and our forgetting Colette, it was exactly two hours after we'd expected to start, but Mother said that wasn't bad at all. And the weather couldn't have been more cooperative if it had tried with both hands. June was cold, so we all had jackets on, with sweaters underneath, and soon we took them off and just had our sweaters. The sun was shining and little clouds were scooting across the sky, and in almost everybody's dooryard there were lilacs blooming.

Daddy said, "Vic, did you bring your guitar?"

Mother said, "Yes," and then, "Heavens, where is it? Suzy and Maggy, if you're sitting on it I shall be in a towering rage."

But John said, "Relax, Mother, I rescued it, it's here with Vicky and me and we're not letting Rob or Rochester use it for a bed."

It takes us the best part of two days and a night to get to Grandfather's, and the trip is part of the fun. We have a special place we like to stop for our picnic lunch. It's about two miles out of our way, up a dirt road in a state park, but it's worth it. There's nothing especially exciting about it; it's just beautiful, and it's sort of a family tradition with us to take our picnic basket there whenever we go to Grandfather's. It's a pine forest, and in the summer, no matter how hot it is, it's always cool there, and in the spring or autumn it's protected and it's never too chilly. We did put our jackets back on, and Mother spread our steamer rug out on the soft, rusty pine needles. All the ground beneath the trees is covered with pine needles, with just an occasional little green bush or seedling growing here and there. The trees are quite close together, so that the bottom branches are rusty-looking, too, and then they get green as they reach up to the sun. The wind was singing in the tops of the pines, so that at first you would almost think it was rushing water. Colette went dashing around in ecstasy as though she were a young puppy. Maybe I ought to have a whole chapter on Colette sometime, but, as Kipling says, that's another story.

We had a lovely picnic, egg-salad sandwiches and sliced lamb sandwiches, and Mother had two big thermos bottles of hot bouillon. When we started off again Rob got in the front seat to sit with Mother and have a nap, and John and I sat on the quilt with the suitcases, and Suzy and Maggy were right, it really wasn't very comfortable unless you lay down, but it was fun looking out the back.

We stopped for the night at a motel, and this is always fun, too. Maggy made five of us instead of four, which complicated matters a little, but Rob slept on a cot in Mother and Daddy's room. We really did get an early start the next morning.

The most fun of all the trip is the boat ride on the *Sister Anne*. Rob says he's going to be the captain of the *Sister Anne* when he grows up, and he gets so excited every time we ride on her that he gets quite white and looks fearfully solemn, the way he always does whenever anything is terribly important to him. The first time he rode on a merry-go-round we thought he was scared sick, but it was only because he thought it was so wonderful that his face had that funny look.

It's a three-hour ride to Seven Bay Island. You stop at two other islands on the way out; Seven Bay is the farthest out to sea of all. Maggy had been to Europe once with her mother, but the island ferry was the biggest boat the rest of us had ever been on, and even Maggy said it seemed much more like a boat than the *Queen Mary*. The *Queen Mary* is like being in an enormous hotel. But when you're on the *Sister Anne* you're on a boat and there's no two ways about it. We stood up in the prow and there was the sea spreading out before us, and long lines of wooded hills on either side. The wind was so strong that it made us catch our breaths, and we closed our jackets tight and the spray blew into our faces. And oh, the lovely smell where the river runs into the sea!

We had sandwiches and chocolate milk on the boat for lunch, and Rob insisted on sharing his with one of the sailors he'd made friends with. After lunch we went and stood in the prow again and pretended we were Norse explorers, seeing the coast of America for the first time.

It was about the middle of the afternoon when we reached Seven Bay Island, and then it's a fifteen-minute drive to where Grandfather lives. His hill and his stable are on the ocean side of the island, quite unlike the pretty little town that is clustered about the big bay where the boat comes in.

We piled out of the boat and back into the car, and we were so excited we couldn't sit still, and Colette and Rochester were excited, too, and Colette yipped her shrillest yip, until Daddy said, "John, Vicky, one of you, hold Colette before she makes me wreck the car."

Grandfather heard the sound of the car coming up the hill and he was out to meet us, and we all fell out of the car and rushed at him until he had to say, "Whoah! Whoah! Don't knock an old man down!" So then we introduced him to Maggy, and he gave Mother a big hug and a kiss, and we all stood around smiling and being happy to be together. Grandfather's stable had been painted with a fresh new coat of barn-red paint since we'd been there last, and Maggy said, kind of dubiously, "Well, it's really the nicest stable I've ever been in."

There's a kind of loft in the stable with six camp beds in it, and all of us children were to sleep there. Mother and Daddy were to have the room where Grandfather usually sleeps. It isn't a very big room, and it has an enormous four-poster bed, seven feet wide by seven and a half feet long, which takes up almost all the space. There's just room to walk around the bed to make it. One side of the room is all a big window, which Grandfather had put in. It has shutters you can close, but when they're open you look down the steep bluffs to the ocean and the only thing that's farther out on the bluff than Grandfather's stable is the lighthouse. Mother and Daddy always look forward to sleeping in the enormous bed, but Mother says that the first couple of nights, even if they close the shutters, she always stays awake for a long time to see the lighthouse light as it swings around. There are no pictures in the room; Grandfather says you can't ask any picture to compete with that view. But on one wall he painted in soft gray Gothic letters: "God is over all things, under all things; outside all; within, but not enclosed; without, but not excluded; above, but not raised up; below, but not depressed; wholly above, presiding; wholly without, embracing; wholly within, filling."

That has always been one of Grandfather's favorite things, so we knew that it was by Hildevert of Lavardin, who wrote it sometime around 1125.

We didn't even go up to our loft to get settled, but went tearing down to the beach with the dogs, leaving Mother and Daddy to sit and talk with Grandfather. It takes quite a while to get down to the beach if you want to go by car, because the road winds around on long hairpin bends and you have to go terribly slowly. But there's a narrow, steep path going right down the bluff. Part of it is steps, and part of it is slippy-slidy path, and you have to hold on to bushes as you go down. Mother and Daddy told John to take care of Rob, and Suzy to take care of Maggy, and Maggy said, "I'm older," and Suzy said, "But I've been down the cliff and you haven't," and Mother told me to take care of my arm and not fall and bump my teeth, and Daddy said we were to be back in an hour and a half and we were not to go wading.

The tide was out and Colette ran tearing up and down the half-moon of beach in the little cove. And then as a wave retreated she would dash after it, barking furiously, and then when a new wave would come lapping into shore she would retreat in terror, squealing, and we all laughed and laughed at her. Rochester behaved just like a puppy and lay down in the shallow water and rolled in the waves and then in the sand and made himself a perfect mess. He always does whenever we go to Grandfather's, but he's shorthaired so it isn't as bad as if it were Colette getting all full of saltwater and sand.

The little ones all wanted to wade, but John said, very firmly, "You all heard Daddy. You'll spoil everything if you disobey him the first thing. And you know it's still too cold. We'd be frozen if we didn't have on our winter jackets. Let's play leapfrog."

So we played leapfrog, and statues, and then we gathered shells, and then the little ones started to build a sand castle for the tide to come into, and John and I wanted to help, but I guess we were all kind of tired because they said it was their castle and they didn't want John and me messing with it any old how, and John and I said we didn't want to mess around with it, we were much too old for boring old sand castles, so there. Of course, we aren't too old for them. I don't think anybody's ever too old for sand castles—Daddy and Mother seem to love to build them. Anyhow, John and I walked down to the edge of the cove and stood looking out over the ocean. If you stand and look where the ocean laps over the curve of the earth and gets lost in the sky, you can't stay cross or tired for very long. John and I stood there, not talking to each other, but feeling very close and somehow very separate at the same time, because the sky and ocean were so vast and we were so small; and John didn't even seem to mind when I reached out and took his hand. John has never been one for holding hands with anybody, even when he was little, but he didn't jerk away, and we stood there together for a long time, hardly hearing the voices of the little ones behind us. Some gulls were waddling around in the next cove. They seem so clumsy when they are on land compared to the way they look when they fly. Rob let out a shout about something, and they took to the air, and then, suddenly, the one I was watching especially swooped down to the water and came up with a fish in its mouth.

John said, "I'm absolutely starved, and by the time we get back to Grandfather's we'll have been gone an hour and a half. Sometimes I wish we had to climb up to get to the beach so we could climb down to get home."

It *was* a hard climb back up. Suzy and Maggy began complaining when we'd hardly even started, and, of course, that set Rob off. John and I practically had to carry him up, and Suzy and Maggy were whining before we got to the top. John took out his handkerchief and wiped their faces and said, "Now, smile."

When we got back to the stable there was a good smell of cooking. Mother had brought a big canned ham and all kinds of other things, and she and Daddy and Grandfather were in the kitchen and it seemed as though all three of them were talking at once. Mother got a pile of sheets and gave them to John and me and told us to go up to the loft and make up five beds, and she told the little ones to set the table.

You get up to the loft by a ladder, so John climbed first and I handed him the sheets, and then I climbed after him. Rochester doesn't approve of the loft at all, because he can't climb the ladder. He has an old red rug that Grandfather always saves to put at the foot of the ladder for him to sleep on, so he can feel close to us all. Colette can climb the ladder, and she's terribly snooty about it, and that makes poor old Rochester feel even worse about having to stay on the ground.

The loft is a lovely, big, bare room that smells of the ocean. It's always filled with light that moves, because it's reflected from the water. There's a line of windows across the ocean side, so there're no pictures there, either. But on the opposite wall Grandfather had painted a poem which we all love. It's by Thomas Browne, another of Grandfather's favorites, and this is what it is:

> *If thou could'st empty all thyself of self,*
> *Like to a shell dishabited,*
> *Then might He find thee on the ocean shelf,*
> *And say, "This is not dead,"*
> *And fill thee with Himself instead.*

But thou art all replete with very thou
And hast such shrewd activity,
That when He comes He says, "This is enow
Unto itself—'twere better let it be,
It is so small and full, there is no room for Me."

I think that poem must have a good influence on us. We always seem more thoughtful of other people when we're at Grandfather's than we are anywhere else. Or maybe it's Grandfather himself. He's always thinking about what will make other people happy, and I don't think anyone could be unhappy around him for very long. Mother said no one could, and that was why he was such a wonderful minister. And he's beautiful to look at, too. He's very tall, like all our family, and thin, not skinny, and he has very white hair, lots of it, and white eyebrows, not wiry and curly like Daddy's and Uncle Douglas's and John's, but soft and thick, and little children love to sit in his lap and smooth them. When he smiles he has wonderful crinkles at the corners of his eyes, and his eyes sort of glint as though the sun were shining through them. And when he is angry it is terrible. John is very much like him, both as a person and in looks.

We finished putting the sheets on the beds, and got the gray army blankets out of the sea chest. We put two on each bed, one folded double-thickness, and the one on top to tuck in. We would be sleeping without pillows. Maggy had wanted to bring her pillow, but Mother said we couldn't bring five pillows, and if one brought a pillow everybody would want to, so Maggy would have to rough it for a change. Maggy loves her creature comforts.

When we were through with the beds John sat down on his. "Vicky," he said solemnly, "have you ever thought how lucky we are?"

I nodded.

"All our family . . . Grandfather . . . and Mother and Daddy. Sometimes I get so mad at you I'd like to hit you—"

"You used to," I interrupted.

But he went on. "But that night when you fell off your bike and came staggering home all bloody, I don't think I've ever felt so awful. And then we get mad at Maggy so often, and we aren't always tactful, like Suzy saying it always makes the grapefruit come out wrong to have five children instead of four. But we have Mother and Daddy, and we have each other, no matter how much we get in each other's hair. Think how lucky that makes us. Think of all the people who get divorces and everything. And even people we know. Not just Dave's parents getting a divorce, but the way Mac and Judy Harris's parents shout at each other. I know it bothers Mac and Jude."

"It bothers me, too, when I'm over there," I said.

"Of course, Mother and Daddy shout some, too," John said, "but it's different. I can't explain why it's different, but it is."

"It certainly is!" I said.

"Mother says she can never stay mad at Daddy, no matter how hard she tries. And Daddy says, '*Stay* mad! You won't even let me *get* mad at you,' and then they laugh. Aren't you sorry for people who don't laugh, Vicky?"

"Yes. And people who don't love music and books."

"And people," John said.

Mother called up from downstairs then. "John! Vicky! Are you asleep up there? Come on down to dinner!"

When Grandfather's alone he eats in the kitchen when it's cold, and out on the porch when it's warm enough. But when we're there Grandfather has a wonderful table. As I've explained, what with the horses' stalls and the books it's an odd sort of house, without the kind of rooms people are used to. And in one of the stalls there's a very long narrow table that goes up against the wall all the way up to the ceiling when it's not being used. But when you want it, it lets down, and there's an old whaling lamp that hangs above it. It hasn't been electrified because there wasn't any electricity on the island at all till about ten years ago, and the island electricity goes off quite often, so Grandfather still keeps a lot of old lamps. Oh, on the underside of the table, which, of course, is what shows when it's up against the wall, is a big long map of the islands. Propped up against the books on one of the shelves is a Hokusai picture of some people crossing a curved bridge in the rain.

The little ones had set the table and we all hurried to it, and said grace, and then we ate as though we'd never seen food before.

When we were just about finished eating, Rob said sleepily, "Grandfather, there was something I've been saving up to ask you, but I've forgotten what it was."

"Well, if you think of it in the middle of the night come and get in bed with me and tell me," Grandfather said.

Daddy laughed. "That was very unwise of you, Father. Rob

will probably take you up on it. If he can't think of what he was going to ask you, he'll think of something else."

"Rob asks silly questions," Maggy said.

"But when you're Rob's age that's how you find out about things," Grandfather told her.

"We picked shells and made a sand castle this afternoon," Rob said. "Grandfather, when you look out over the ocean you can't see where the sky stops. Does the sky have any end, Grandfather?"

"Well, the clouds and our atmosphere have an end. Then there's space."

"But that's still sky, too, really, isn't it?" Suzy asked.

"In a way."

"But it must have *some* end," Rob said.

"It's a bit of a question, Rob," Grandfather said. "People used to think space went on and on forever, but now they think it's curved, and that it's finite. That means space *does* have an end."

"Grandfather," Rob said, "if it ends, what's beyond that?"

"Even Einstein couldn't give the answer to that one," Grandfather said.

"My father knows," Maggy said. "His airplane exploded and he went out into space and he's living on another star now and he knows everything. John explained it all to me."

John looked rather defensive and opened his mouth as though to speak, but Grandfather said quietly, "John knows that God has taken care of your father."

Suzy said, "I'd like to know everything in the world."

"It's more than everything in the world, though, Suzy," Grandfather said. "It's become much bigger than that. The

190

search for knowledge and truth can be the most exciting thing there is as long as it takes you toward God instead of away from Him."

"Einstein didn't believe in God," John said.

"Oh, didn't he! Excuse me, Victoria, Wallace," and Grandfather got up from the table and we could hear him hurrying into another of the stalls. He came back in just a moment with a book and he almost glared at John as he said, "Now, listen here, young John, to Einstein's own words," and he read:

> " 'The scientist's religious feeling takes the form of a rapturous amazement at the harmony of natural law, which reveals an intelligence of such superiority that, compared with it, all the systematic thinking and acting of human beings is utterly insignificant reflection. This feeling is the guiding principle of his life and work, in so far as he succeeds in keeping himself from the shackles of selfish desire. It is beyond question closely akin to that which has possessed the religious geniuses of all ages.' "

He closed the book and sat down. "And you say Einstein didn't believe in God!"

John stood up and bowed. "I stand corrected," he said, took the big blue pitcher, and filled his milk glass for at least the fourth time.

Grandfather took a bite of chocolate cake, then opened the book and started looking through it again. "Listen to this," he said, and he was so interested in what he wanted to read to us that he was talking with his mouth full: " 'The true value of a human being is determined primarily by the measure and the sense in which he has attained liberation from self.' " He let his glasses slip off the end of his nose and looked at us. He only uses reading glasses, not thick lenses like John. "Isn't that the teaching of Jesus? Isn't that the meaning of the poem in the loft? And listen to this:

" 'What is the meaning of human life, or, for that matter, of the life of any creature? To know an answer to this question means to be religious. You ask: Does it make any sense, then, to post this question? I answer: The man who regards his own life and that of his fellow creatures as meaningless is not merely unhappy but hardly fit for life.' "

Then Grandfather smiled rather sheepishly at us all. "Well, children, I'm sorry, but John brought it on."

I know the little ones didn't understand what he was reading, because I didn't understand all of it myself. I knew it was important, and I knew that for some reason it made me feel happy.

"Do you think I'd understand that book?" John asked.

"Some of it," Grandfather told him. "Why don't you try it?"

Somehow none of us really felt like talking very much after what Grandfather had read, and anyhow, we were all very full and very sleepy.

Mother said, "All right, my darlings, up that ladder and into bed. Grandfather and Daddy and I will do the dishes and you get to sleep as fast as you can. I'll come up and kiss you and tuck you in later on."

We didn't argue about staying up later. I think Rob was asleep even before he got into bed. He didn't get under the covers, he just flopped down on the cot in his flannel pajamas, and when John said, "Get into bed, Rob," he didn't move, he was sound asleep.

Suzy said, "He's playing possum."

But John said, "Not this time," and picked him up and put him under the covers and tucked him in.

There were rattan blinds at our windows, but we didn't pull them down. We lay there and it was a completely different dark from the dark at home, and every minute it was broken by the finger of light from the lighthouse sweeping across our beds. I thought it might keep me awake, but it didn't.

It was one of the nicest vacations we've ever had. We spent the days on the beach and the weather was perfect, sunny, and as long as you stayed in the sun, quite warm, though chillish if you got out of it. One of the best things about it was that there wasn't ever any rush. No one had to hurry to get anywhere. In the mornings we could all sleep as late as we liked, and so could Mother and Daddy. And when we heard them stirring we could go down and get into the enormous bed with them and talk and laugh and be comfortable. For lunches we usually had picnics, and then there were the dinners at the long table, sometimes just the family and sometimes with a friend or two of Grandfather's. And then when we went up to bed there was the arm of light sweeping across our beds, and seeming, like the sea wind, to sweep everything clean and pure. And the sound of laughter coming up from below, and almost always, last of all, the sound of the guitar, and Mother singing.

When it came time for Mother and Daddy to go and it was half over for all of us it seemed as though we could hardly bear it. We wanted it to last forever just the way it was, but Grandfather said wonderful things couldn't last forever, or they would be dulled by repetition and cease being wonderful.

On Mother and Daddy's last night with us, we all drove down to the beach and sat in the shelter of Grandfather's cove and watched the moon rise. I'd never realized how different the moon is rising over the mountains and rising over the sea. At first there was just a hint of light out over the horizon, and then the crust of the moon seemed to pull itself up right out of the water, and it was a deep, deep yellow, almost orange, and sort of flattened at the top. And it looked terribly *old,* and strange, and John said, "If our earth didn't have any moon there wouldn't be any tides, would there? I suppose the ocean would be quite different if there weren't any tides."

That was a spooky idea to me, having the familiar ocean be quite different, and sitting there, leaning against Daddy, I shivered.

But Daddy said, laughing, "Think of the planets that have more than one moon! Think how confused their oceans must get."

Mother laughed, too, and said, "Just like me, with lots of children constantly pulling me this way and that!"

Rob started to chant, "I'm a little moon, I'm a little moon," and then we were all laughing.

All in a moment the moon fairly seemed to leap up out of the ocean like a porpoise, and as it leaped up into the sky it lost its weird orangy look and grew round and clear and white. Rob said, "I see the man in the moon and he's laughing at us!"

It really seemed that we *could* see an impish face up there laughing down at us!

Mother and Grandfather began singing,

> "The man in the moon
> Came down too soon
> And asked the way to Norwich.
> He went by the south
> And burned his mouth
> With eating cold plum porridge."

"I just don't *get* it," Maggy said, as she always did when Mother sang that song. "How could he burn his mouth if it was *cold* plum porridge?"

"I want plum porridge for breakfast," Rob said sleepily. "I never had any."

Right after breakfast the next morning Mother and Daddy left. Daddy was going to go to a medical convention in New York as well as everything else, and it made a very good thing to tell the little ones, so they didn't have to worry about Maggy's fate being settled. Daddy warned John and me again that Mr. Ten Eyck was perfectly capable of thinking our open, country life wasn't at all the thing he wanted for his granddaughter. He was strictly a city person and he could very easily think the way we lived was much too free and easy and that Maggy needed lots more polish than she would get with us. And when Daddy talked like that about it we didn't feel as sure as we had about everything all that first beautiful week at the island.

We all stood outside the stable and waved and waved, long after the station wagon had disappeared around the bend in the road and we couldn't see Mother and Daddy any longer, as though they'd be gone for much more than a week.

We all had various duties for the week we were to be there without Mother and Daddy. John and I were to do the cooking. I was really in charge, but John was to help me as much as he could and take care of the picnics. And he was to sweep the floors every morning before we went down to the beach or did whatever was planned for the day, while Suzy and Maggy and I did the breakfast dishes and made the beds. John's sweeping was quite a job, because on an island lots of sea sand gets tracked in. Rob was to do anything Grandfather asked him to do, like going over to the neighbors' with a basket for eggs. And, of course, John and I were strictly responsible for the younger ones at the beach, and they'd promised never to go wading or anything like that unless we were along.

Everything started out all smoothly and beautifully. We all did our jobs without squawking—even Maggy; I guess Grandfather and the island had a good influence on her, too.

Then there came a Day.

It scares me to think of it even now.

It was the hottest day we'd had, and the little ones kept begging to go swimming, but John and I said no, only wading, and they weren't to get their clothes wet, either.

We cooked hot dogs out on the beach for lunch and then right after lunch John went back to the stable to work on a summer book report; and after a while Suzy went on back, because she was still hungry and she wanted to make herself a peanut-butter-and-jelly sandwich. Rob and Maggy and I were building a sand castle for the tide to come into, and when that was finished Rob and Maggy went off to collect shells. I had more shells than I knew what to do with already, so I climbed up on a rock and started reading a book I'd brought down in the picnic basket. It was low tide, which is the best time for finding good shells, and Maggy and Rob kept coming back and dumping shells at my feet, some of them quite pretty, but most of them just plain shells like the boxes and baskets of shells they already had up in the loft. In Grandfather's cove there is a long spit of land that goes like a path out into the ocean. It's covered when the tide is high, but when it's low tide you can always find the best shells of all on it. So Rob and Maggy kept running up and down the path of sand and shrieking with delight each time they saw a special shell.

After a while I heard my name being called, and then there was Suzy peering around the rocks.

"Vicky," she said anxiously, "something's the matter with Colette, and she just yips and snaps when I try to go near her."

"What's wrong?" I asked.

"I don't know; she won't let me look. She keeps batting at her face with her paw, and then she rubs her face on the floor, and she's whining and whimpering. John said I'd better get you."

"You mean she won't bite the hand that feeds her?" I asked. One of my jobs is feeding Colette and Rochester, so Colette does have a special feeling for me. "Okay, I'll come. C'mon, Maggy and Rob."

"Oh, leave them," Suzy said impatiently. "We don't want a lot of people hovering around Colette, especially if . . . Vicky, you don't think she could have hydrophobia, do you?"

"No, I don't," I said; but the idea had crossed my mind. I thought hard for a minute.

Maggy and Rob were having a wonderful time, and they didn't want to leave and climb up the path to the stable, so I finally told them I was going back up for just a few minutes. "But stay in Grandfather's cove," I warned them, "and don't do any more wading till John or I come back. Why don't you build another sand castle? The tide's starting to come in. Or you can look for more shells. Or—"

"Come *on,* Vic," Suzy urged.

"Okay, I'll be back down in just a little while," I told them, and followed Suzy up the cliff.

When we got back up to the stable Colette was in the kitchen with John watching her, looking very upset. And she was certainly acting very peculiarly. She had her head down on the floor and she was moaning, and then she flopped down and rubbed at her jaws with both paws. It would have been funny if it hadn't been pathetic, and sort of scary, too. Then she started running around in circles, and I got really frightened, because I'd read in a book about a mad dog running around in circles. I went to the sink and filled Colette's water bowl.

"What are you doing that for?" John asked.

"I want to see if she's thirsty," I said. I didn't explain that I'd just remembered that hydrophobia means fear of water. I put the bowl down by Colette and she sniffed at it but wouldn't drink any, and then she began batting at her face again.

I sat down on the floor by her and talked to her softly. "Colly, Colette, c'mere, Colly, come to Vicky." She did come to me, though I hadn't really expected her to, moaning piteously. Tentatively I put my hand to her jaws, but she jerked away, then came back to me again. She did this two or three times, but she didn't really go away from me or start to run around in circles again. She rubbed her head hard against my knee, and finally I took my courage in both hands and held her tight and stuck my fingers in her mouth. She gave an awful yelp and sort of snapped at me, but I'd discovered what was wrong.

I looked up at John and Suzy in relief. "It's one of those lamb-chop bones I gave her last night. She's got a piece of it wedged up in the roof of her mouth. Hold her tight for me so she can't wiggle away." John and Suzy held Colette, and I managed to reach in and dislodge the chop bone. And then Colette was all over me, licking my face to thank me, and she stood up on her hind paws and waved her front paws and begged.

"Give her a biscuit," Suzy said.

"A biscuit's so hard," I said, "and I'm sure the roof of her mouth is sore." What Colette loves more than anything in the world is buttered toast, so I told John and Suzy I was going to make her some, and they decided to have some, too. As a matter of fact, we were hungry again. Colette danced about, delighted at having got rid of the chop bone, and ate pieces of all our buttered toast. Then we had some tea, and Colette had several saucersful, with lots of milk.

After a while John said, "I hope Rob and Maggy are okay."

"Well, of course they are!" Suzy said impatiently. "Maggy's old enough to look after Rob for a few minutes."

"I hope you told them not to go wading," John said anxiously, like a mother hen.

"What do you think I am!" I said indignantly. "I've got *some* sense of responsibility."

"Sure, Vic," John said, "but I'll just feel better if you'll go down and check on them."

I thought I'd feel better, too, so I slithered down the cliff path to Grandfather's cove. And they weren't there. There was the sand castle they had been building, and there were two more big piles of shells, but no sign of either of them. "I *told* them not to go out of Grandfather's cove!" I said aloud.

I wasn't very worried yet, though, and I clambered around the rocks to the bigger cove where we sometimes go but they weren't there, either. I went back to Grandfather's cove. *Make* them be there, I half thought, half prayed, and I really thought I'd see them squatting by the sand castle or playing with their shells. But they weren't there. The picnic basket was there, and the thermos jug of lemonade, and my book, but no Rob or Maggy. I called and called but nobody answered except a gull. The tide was well on its way in now, and a good half of the spit of land where they'd been trotting up and down getting shells was already underwater. I began to feel panicky. I put the book in the picnic basket, carried the basket in one hand and the heavy thermos jug in the other, and clambered back up the cliff-side to the stable.

In the stable all was peace and quiet. Grandfather was writing at his desk with Colette sleeping peacefully at his feet, and he looked so happy and busy that I hated to disturb him, especially with something worrying, so I climbed the ladder to the loft, but nobody was there. Then I heard a noise in the kitchen, so I hurried down.

Please make Rob and Maggy be there. Make them have come home without my knowing it.

But just John and Suzy were there, both of them eating more toast and marmalade.

"Where're Rob and Maggy?" John asked.

"They aren't there," I said flatly. "They aren't in Grandfather's cove or anywhere around. I called and called and they didn't answer."

"Where could they be?" Suzy asked blankly.

John looked at me and said, "Mother and Daddy said we were never to leave the little ones at the beach without one of us being there."

"John, *don't!*" I cried. "Help me find them!"

"All right," John said. "The first thing is not to get panicky. They're undoubtedly perfectly all right. We've just got to figure out where they're likely to be. Just where did you leave them, Vicky?"

"In Grandfather's cove," I said again. "I told them to stay right there till I came back for them and they weren't to go near the water."

"And she really wasn't gone very long," Suzy said in my defense. "Just while she took the chop bone out of Colette's mouth and made the tea and toast. And if they didn't want to stay down at the beach I don't see why they didn't come back up to the stable."

"I don't think Rob would go off and do anything cockeyed by himself," John said. "I'm sure of Rob, and I thought I was sure of Maggy, but now that it comes to the point, I'm not quite so sure. I'm trying to think, well, what would Maggy, being Maggy, be most likely to do, and I don't know."

"Could they have gone to the post office?" Suzy suggested.

"But you remember, we all walked to the post office this morning."

"Oh. Well, they wouldn't have gone there."

"I want to look for them," I said nervously. "I don't want to sit here and talk about it."

"The point is," John said, "we have to figure out where to look. There's no point going off half cocked to the post office if they've gone in the other direction. You really looked thoroughly on the beach, Vic?"

"Of *course*."

"Do you think we ought to tell Grandfather?" Suzy asked.

"Not yet." John shook his head. "Okay, Vic, it's not that I don't trust you, but I'm going to look down on the beach again."

"But I *did*——" I started to protest.

"I know, but they might have wandered off and come back," John said. "You go look over by the lighthouse. Suzy, you stay here, and if they come back you tell us as fast as you can.

Vicky and I'll be as quick as possible and we'll meet right back here."

I half ran, half walked, along the narrow cliff road. Above me the sea gulls had evidently sighted some fish or something that excited them, because they kept diving and swooping and crying, and I kept thinking it was Rob or Maggy, crying or frightened or hurt. When I got to the yellow frame building across the road from the lighthouse where Mr. Henreys, the lighthouse keeper, and his wife lived, I went in and asked if they had seen Rob or Maggy anywhere that afternoon, and they hadn't. So I turned around and hurried back to the stable again. The thing that kept bothering me, the thing that for some reason I kept seeing in my mind, was Rob and Maggy walking out on that spit of land hunting for shells, and knowing now that the spit of land was rapidly being covered with water from the incoming tide; and Rob is too young to swim much and I didn't even know whether Maggy could swim or not.

Suzy was waiting for me in the kitchen. She said she'd just gone up to the loft to look out; she'd seen me on my way back from the lighthouse, and John starting up the cliff path, and she could see all along the beach, but there was no sign of Rob or Maggy.

"But I couldn't have seen them, of course," she said, "if they'd been around the corner of a cove or behind a rock."

"It's my fault," I said. "I told them I'd be right back."

"There isn't any point in *blaming* anybody," Suzy said. "If it comes to blame, we told them to stay right where they were, and they didn't."

John came in then. "They aren't down at the beach and that's that." He looked at me and I looked at him and neither of us said what we were thinking.

"The tide's coming in," Suzy said. "If they went into some of the littler coves they couldn't get back to Grandfather's cove until the tide goes out again. Rob's too little to climb up the cliff except by the path."

"Well, maybe we'd better not just go on looking by ourselves," John said, sort of tentatively. "Maybe we'd better tell Grandfather."

"Tell Grandfather what?" a voice asked, and Maggy came strolling into the kitchen.

"Maggy!" We all pounced on her, the three of us shouting at once, where had she been, why hadn't they stayed in Grandfather's cove the way I told them to, why had they worried us that way, and then, all of a sudden, "Where's Rob?"

Maggy looked blank. "Rob? Isn't he with you?"

"He was with *you!*" I said fiercely. "I left you with him in Grandfather's cove and you *knew* you should have stayed there till I got back. You're six years older than Rob! You *knew* you were in charge of him!"

"You didn't tell me I was," Maggy said.

At that point I would gladly have seen Maggy thrown to the lions.

"She didn't have to tell you," John said coldly. "Where have you been and why did you leave Rob?"

Maggy looked around from one to the other of us, her vague look slowly being replaced by a wary one; if there was anything Maggy hated, it was acknowledging she'd done wrong in any way—hated it even more than the rest of us. Finally she said, "Well, Rob told me to go away, so I went."

"No, Maggy, that won't do," John said.

"Well, what really happened," Maggy started again, "was that we were playing hide-and-seek and it was my turn to hide and, well . . . and . . . and I waited and waited and when Rob didn't come look for me I . . . well . . . I thought he'd come back to the stable, so I came along to see if he was here. I was . . . I was looking for him."

Suzy came up to Maggy and looked at her earnestly. Suzy is a full year younger than Maggy, but they're just exactly the same size, and Suzy looked her right in the eyes. "Maggy, do you remember Wilbur the pig?"

"Well, sure," Maggy said. "Why?"

"And right after that I took the candy from the Jenkins' store and I didn't tell Mother or Daddy or anything and when Mother and Daddy asked if I knew anything about the candy I said no and I didn't tell the truth?"

Maggy got very pink, but all she said was, "Well, sure I remember."

"And I remember *you* said you never lied."

"Well, I never do."

"Then please *don't*," Suzy begged. "We know Rob loves to play tricks, and when he's mad at people he does say 'Go away,' but he'd never have left you like that after Vicky told you to stay together in Grandfather's cove. Please, Maggy, all we want to know is where to look for Rob. You've *got* to help us. Why aren't you with Rob and why didn't you stay in Grandfather's cove?"

"Well, we *were* playing hide-and-seek," Maggy said. "Honestly."

"Okay," John said. "We all believe you were playing hide-and-seek. Then what?"

"Then—well, then nothing."

John suddenly looked terribly old and grownup. "We'll have to go to Grandfather," he said.

Then I had an idea. "Maggy, did *you* play the trick on Rob? Did *you* go off and leave *him* for a joke?"

Maggy nodded.

"Then what happened?" John asked. "Maggy, please! You've got to tell us right away! Don't you realize, every minute you pussyfoot around something awful might happen to Rob? He can't swim very well, and the tide's coming in."

All the pink went out of Maggy's cheeks and she went very white and the darks of her eyes seemed to get very big. When she spoke it was breathlessly, as though John had hit her in the stomach. "It was just for a joke. It was Rob's turn to hide, so I climbed up the cliff path and then I walked on down to Dick's Place and had an ice-cream cone. I had a dime in my pocket."

"And you knew if Rob came along you'd have to share it with him!" Suzy said furiously.

But John shushed her warningly.

"And when I got back he was gone," Maggy said. "That's the honest truth. I thought he'd just grown tired of waiting for me and come back to the stable. So I waded for a few minutes to cool my feet off, and then I went and picked some kind of pink flower for Grandfather—it was blooming all over the path—and then I just came along home."

This time we knew she was telling us the truth. John said, "Okay, Maggy, thanks. But we've got to tell Grandfather that we don't know where Rob is. Vicky and I've both looked down at the beach and Vicky went to the lighthouse and now we don't know where he could be and he's too young to be wandering off somewhere by himself."

"The tide's coming in," Suzy said again.

John said, "Suzy, shut *up!*"

Then he led the way to Grandfather's desk.

Grandfather listened gravely, one hand slowly stroking Colette's ear. He looked down at Colette, then at us, and then he asked, "Where's Mr. Rochester?"

None of us knew where Mr. Rochester was. Maggy said he hadn't come down to the beach while she and Rob were still playing there. But Grandfather said in his quiet way, "Mr. Rochester must be with Rob now, and we all know that Mr. Rochester will take care of him." He spoke with such assurance that we couldn't help feeling better, and yet John and I knew that he was worried, because somehow, without any line or expression in his face being altered, he suddenly looked older. "I'd better make some telephone calls," he said.

We stood by while he phoned, first to the people round about that we knew, the Nortons who had the big house down the hill the stable had once belonged to, the Woods who took us out in their boat, everybody Rob might have gone to see; but nobody had seen him. Then Grandfather called in to the village, the post office, the grocer and the butcher and the drugstore, old Mrs. Adams who played the organ at the church, and

Reverend Mr. Hanchett, though Rob wasn't apt to be there, because although we all loved Mr. Hanchett, Mrs. Hanchett was, as Grandfather said, a very peculiar woman more like a hatchet than a Hanchett, and among other things she didn't like children or dogs, so neither Rob nor Mr. Rochester would have had too warm a welcome there.

And nobody had seen him.

Grandfather sat with his hand over the receiver of the phone as though he was terribly, terribly tired. Then he phoned the Coast Guard.

We just stood there, and then we realized that Maggy must have slipped out, and Suzy went out to the kitchen to look for her, and John looked in all the stalls, and I went up to the loft, and she was lying face down on her bed, not moving, just lying there.

I hated myself, I hated Maggy, though I was no longer ready to send her to the lions, and I was so full of panic that I was shivering all over. I stood there and looked at her until I could make myself speak, and then I said, "Maggy, let's all go down to the Coast Guard headquarters and wait."

Grandfather said we might go, but he would stay by the phone in case Rob turned up at somebody's house or something.

We hurried along, not speaking, until John said, "I had to get out, I had to do something, I couldn't just sit there and wait. But one of us should have stayed with Grandfather. We shouldn't have left him to wait there all alone."

"If it's bad news, maybe he'd rather *be* alone," Suzy said in a gritty sort of voice.

"Mr. *Rochester's* with Rob!" I cried. "You *know* Mr. Rochester wouldn't let anything happen to Rob!"

"How do you know he's with Rob?"

"Where else would he be? Mr. Rochester *never* goes off by himself. He's *always* with one of us if he isn't at home."

At the Coast Guard office they spoke to us kindly. "Why don't you go down and look everywhere in the village, kids?"

"But Grandfather called everywhere," John said.

"I know, but your little brother just might turn up, and if you find him, you call *us* right away."

So we went on down to the village. We asked in every house, even the houses where we didn't know the people, and one woman slammed the door in our faces, but everybody else was very nice to us, and some of them were too nice and I almost started to cry. John saw that I was almost crying after we'd been talking to one lady who asked us lots of questions and then called us "poor little things," and he grabbed my arm and pressed it so hard that it hurt and he whispered fiercely, "Vicky, don't! You can't!" And I didn't.

At the drugstore the druggist asked us, "Did you go down to the dock? You know how crazy your little brother is about that boat."

"No," John said. "Why didn't we think of it! And Grandfather didn't phone there!"

Mr. Ross picked up his phone and asked if anybody at the dock had seen a small boy wandering about by himself, but nobody had.

Then it was almost worse than before. When Mr. Ross mentioned the dock I was suddenly sure that that was where

Rob had gone, and then to be disappointed like that made me feel all hollow with fear. But I said, "Let's go down to the dock anyhow. Let's just look around. They mightn't have noticed him. You know how Rob can sit off in a corner and just watch, quiet as a little mouse."

So we went down to the dock. We didn't have much hope, but it gave us one more thing to do, and we didn't want to go back to the Coast Guard office too soon.

Suzy said with her horrible insistence on realism, "The *Sister Anne* went out an hour ago at least. He wouldn't still be there."

"But he *might* be," I persisted. "The dockhands are always doing something down around the dock that he'd like to watch."

There were a couple of dockhands lounging outside the big white rickety-looking ferry terminal, but they didn't stop us or ask us what we were doing when we went inside. There wasn't another boat coming to the island that day; there's only the one that gets in about three in the afternoon and gets back to the mainland around six, so there weren't many people around. We went through the big building and out onto the slip where the *Sister Anne* comes in, and there, sitting on his haunches and looking out to sea, was Mr. Rochester!

How we rushed at him! How we hugged him! But he couldn't talk, he couldn't tell us where Rob was or why he was just sitting there. He greeted us happily, wagging his whole body and giving us big wet kisses, and I cried, "It's all right! He wouldn't be glad to see us if anything awful had happened to Rob!"

We asked everybody we could find, but they all said they hadn't seen any little boy wandering about alone.

"We'll go back to the Coast Guard," John said, "and tell them we've found Rochester."

We called Rochester to come along with us, but he wouldn't move. He wagged, but when we tried to get him to follow us, he just sat down again and looked out to sea.

So we left him and ran all the way to the Coast Guard headquarters. I got a terrible stitch in my side, but I kept on running, and I thought that probably the others had stitches, too, and Maggy was panting horribly, and John kept having to push his glasses back up his nose, but we just kept on running till we got there.

"There isn't any news, kids," they told us. "You'd better go home and wait with your grandfather." Their voices were serious and kind.

"But Mr. Rochester's sitting down at the boat slip waiting!" We all started to talk at once.

"Okay, now, one at a time," the man who seemed to be in charge said to us; we found out later he was Commander Rodney. "You tell me what this is about, son." He spoke to John. "Who is this mister whoever he is?"

"Mr. Rochester is our Great Dane," John said. "He's a very reliable dog. And he disappeared about the same time Rob did, so we knew he must be with Rob. And Rob is crazy about the *Sister Anne,* so we went down to the dock and onto the slip and Mr. Rochester was sitting there, looking out to sea. He was glad to see us but he wouldn't come with us, he just insisted on staying there looking out after where the *Sister Anne* must have gone."

The Commander said, "A stowaway, maybe? Hold on." He reached for his telephone and called the dock, but they told him the same thing they had told Mr. Ross when he called from the drugstore and that they had told us when we asked: they hadn't seen any little boy wandering around loose. But they did go look and they said that a large dog was still sitting there at the edge of the slip, but, although he wagged his tail, he wouldn't let anybody near him.

The Commander said, "Okay, kids, wait here. I'm going to go speak to my telegraph officer." He went off and while he was gone another man came in and gave us all Cokes. We drank them to be polite, and we were thirsty and dry from all the running we'd done, and under any other circumstances a Coke would have tasted wonderful, but we couldn't really enjoy it.

The Commander was gone for what seemed like forever. The nice man who brought us the Cokes joked with us and asked questions and I guess he was trying to get our minds off things, but they wouldn't get off. I kept pressing my knuckles up against my lips to try to keep from showing how they were trembling and how frightened I was, and John answered all the questions in a rigid sort of voice that didn't sound like John at all, and Suzy kept stalking to the window and looking out as though she thought maybe she could find Rob that way, and Maggy just sat there with her fists clenched and didn't say a word.

The Commander came back in and he was grinning and he said, "Well, kids, your Mr. What's-his-name knew the score. Your little brother is on the *Sister Anne*."

Maggy dashed to him and flung her arms around his neck and kissed him, crying out, "Oh, you're just wonderful. I just love you!"

John said, "Could we call Grandfather?"

Suzy said, "I want to buy Rochester the biggest steak on the island."

I couldn't say anything at all because I was trying so hard not to cry with relief and happiness.

"Lieutenant Andrews is calling your grandfather," the Commander said.

"But how did Rob *get* on the *Sister Anne?*" Suzy asked.

The Commander laughed. "There was a family with seven children getting on, and he just attached himself to them and nobody even noticed him, not even the parents. As the father of only four children, I can see how this would be perfectly possible! He was playing quite happily with the children up on deck and everybody thought he belonged to somebody else."

"Well, how is he going to get *off* the *Sister Anne?*" Suzy asked. "She doesn't come back till tomorrow afternoon."

The Commander ran his fingers through his grizzly, graying hair. I guess all fathers of four or more children have graying hair. "We're sending a cutter out for him. And then I would suggest that he be spanked hard and put to bed without dinner."

He said it kindly and with a twinkle, but I felt I should explain that it was my fault, so I tried to. Then Maggy said it was her fault, and finally the Commander shooed us off and said we'd better get back to Grandfather.

We all went to meet Rob as he came in off the cutter. They brought him in at the *Sister Anne*'s slip instead of the Coast

Guard headquarters because of Mr. Rochester. They were really very understanding people. Mr. Rochester practically knocked Rob down with his welcome, and then he tried to thank the Coast Guard men by putting his feet on their shoulders and kissing their faces, and Grandfather had to call him down. The Commander was there and he drove us home, and he tried to scold Rob, but he didn't sound cross at all, and Rob was so excited about his ride in the cutter he didn't even know he was being scolded.

When we got back to the stable and after we'd all finished thanking the Commander, Grandfather took Rob into the stall that is his study and sent the rest of us into the kitchen to get dinner. I made Sloppy Joe because that's quick and everybody likes it, and we had some hamburger in the refrigerator, and Suzy and Maggy set the table, and John filled and trimmed the lamps. Then Grandfather and Rob came out, hand in hand, Rob not saying anything at all, and we went in to dinner.

We held hands around the table for our family grace, and then Grandfather said in a voice loud and glad:

> "O come, let us sing unto the Lord,
> Let us make a joyful noise to the rock of our salvation.
> Let us come before His presence with Thanksgiving,
> And make a joyful noise unto Him with psalms."

And then suddenly the week was over and we were back down at the slip waiting for Mother and Daddy to come in on the *Sister Anne*. Rob was the first one to spot the boat, and there it was, just a far-off speck at first, and then coming closer and whiter and bigger until we could see the black specks of people on deck and leaning at the railings; and then there she was, coming into the slip, and we could see Mother and Daddy, and with them, oh, lovely surprise, was Uncle Douglas!

It had only been a week since we'd seen Mother and Daddy but we'd never been away from them for so long before, and it seemed as though it had been months and months. Then the glorious moment came when they were off the boat and there was a tangle of arms and suitcases and everybody hugging and jumping up and down, and then two of the sailors came looking for Rob and took him off to see the captain, and Mother and Daddy and Uncle Douglas had to be told all about his trip on the *Sister Anne* and how terrified we had been till we found out where he was. And then at last we were all in the station wagon on the way back to Grandfather's stable and everybody was talking at once and it was all loud and noisy and happy and right.

When we got back to Grandfather's the Woods were waiting for us to take us out for one last ride on their boat, and instead of taking us right home afterward they said they had an order from Grandfather to pick up something he wanted for dinner, and they took us to the part of the island called Johnson's Neck where the fishermen's boats come in, and bought lobsters right off the boat.

At dinner Mother and Daddy told us all about their time in New York. They'd gone to concerts and plays but, of course, the main thing we wanted to know about was Maggy. We could tell from their faces that it was all right, that she wasn't going to be thrown to the lions, so we could relax and listen while

Mother and Daddy and Uncle Douglas told us all about their conferences with Mr. Ten Eyck. The luckiest thing, I guess, was that Mr. Ten Eyck was very enthusiastic about Uncle Douglas's portrait of Maggy's mother. And Uncle Douglas said he'd surprised himself, because he liked the portrait, too, even though he doesn't like painting that way, from photographs, especially knowing so much was at stake.

Uncle Douglas had suggested that both Mr. Ten Eyck, as Maggy's closest of kin, and Aunt Elena, to fulfill Maggy's father's wish, be made legal guardians, and Mr. Ten Eyck consented to this and so did the judge at the probate court. They all went down there to talk with the judge and everything was arranged; the judge decided that it was best for Maggy not to be brought into court, since everybody agreed about her and he thought she'd been through enough already. It all turned out to be much more informal than they'd been afraid it might.

Of course, Maggy, being Maggy, said, "But I'd like to have gone to court. I've never been in court and talked to a judge."

"The judge was little and skinny and I don't think he'd have impressed you at all," Uncle Douglas told her.

"And am I going to stay with you?" Maggy demanded of Daddy. "I know Aunt Elena can't keep me and I don't want to live with Grandpa. I want to stay with you because you're my family now."

"Yes, Maggy," Daddy told her. "You're to continue to live with us, just as you've been doing."

"Well, that's okay, then," Maggy said. "May Suzy and I be excused now?"

* * *

When the little ones were in bed, with Uncle Douglas in the loft reading *Doctor Dolittle* to them, Daddy said to John and me, "Of course, if Aunt Elena should remarry, as one day she probably will, I imagine she'll want to have Maggy with her then."

I couldn't help saying, as I'd said once before, "Daddy, don't you think Uncle Douglas is in love with Aunt Elena?"

John said, "I think he has been for years. You know that."

"Well, wouldn't it really be wonderful if they ended up getting married?" I asked.

"Still at it!" Mother said, and laughed. "You're both incorrigible."

"Yes, but wouldn't it?"

Daddy said, "Uncle Douglas knows that things like that can't be rushed, children. I trust you'll keep your ideas on the subject strictly to yourselves."

"Of course!" John said. "But, Dad, it wouldn't matter that Uncle Douglas is younger than Aunt Elena, would it?"

"When people are compatible, a few years' difference one way or the other doesn't matter much. I'm five years older than Mother."

"Now, matchmakers," Mother said briskly, "we're going to try to make an early start tomorrow morning. It's time you went off to the loft, too."

So it was the last night in the loft, though it didn't seem possible that two weeks had passed so quickly and so much had happened. I sat up in my cot and looked out the window and listened to the ocean and smelled the wonderful sea wind and saw and *felt* the golden bar of light from the lighthouse sweeping over me until I was so sleepy that I had to lie down and go to sleep.

And then, the next morning, it was time to leave Grandfather, and oh, how we always hate to leave him! When we left, he stood on the steps and waved and waved to us and the sun shone on his lovely white hair and we all looked back and waved and waved until we couldn't see him any more.

Then, on the way home, we had another wonderful thing, a surprise for all of us, for a celebration.

"We'll go home by a different way this time," Daddy said. "We haven't been to Boston for a long time."

We got to Boston in the late afternoon and took baths and went for a walk on the Common and fed the swans and then went and had a lovely roast-beef dinner at our hotel, and then, when we expected to be sent up to bed, Mother and Daddy told us that they were going to take us to Symphony Hall to hear the orchestra, because we didn't get many chances at home to hear live music, and no matter how wonderful our records are, they're still canned.

We all went, even Rob. John and I started in looking at our programs, and John said, giving me a poke so big that I thought he'd broken one of my ribs, "Hey!"

"What in the——" I started.

But John said, "*Look,* Vic!" And he pointed to his program and underneath the symphony and the conductor there was Aunt Elena's name! She was to be the soloist with the orchestra and to play Rachmaninoff's *Second Piano Concerto!*

Mother and Daddy and Uncle Douglas were smiling enormous smiles and Maggy let out a squeal and people turned around to look, so we all calmed down, and then the members of the orchestra started coming out on the stage and Mother told us to be quiet and watch and listen. Rob and Suzy had never seen a whole orchestra before, and neither John nor I had many times, and it's one of the most exciting things I know about, particularly as they start tuning up. It isn't music, the sounds that the instruments make as they catch their note, but to me it's very beautiful.

Finally the conductor came out and everybody applauded and then the house settled down into silence and the conductor raised his baton and the music began. They started with Handel's *Royal Fireworks Music*. This is something Mother plays on the phonograph quite often, so we all knew it, and she was right: it did sound very different to us, sitting there, with the music flowing out at us from the stage, surrounding us, filling us—yes, it was quite different from when we listen to the record at home.

But, of course, the exciting moment was when Aunt Elena came out onto the stage. She wore a long black dress and her neck and shoulders and face shone out very white between the dress and her hair.

Her music was very different from the *Fireworks Music*. The *Fireworks Music* is gay, and even if I'm depressed when I start listening to it, I end up by wanting to get up and dance. But in the middle of the Rachmaninoff I suddenly felt so sad, though it was a sort of beautiful sadness, that I wanted to clutch Mother and Daddy for comfort and cry and cry.

When Aunt Elena finished playing, the applause was

219

almost like a thunderstorm, it was so violent, and I looked over at Mother and she was sitting there, clapping and smiling with tears in her eyes because she was so moved by the music and so proud of Aunt Elena.

Then we all went back to the hotel and up to Aunt Elena's suite to have supper with her, and Aunt Elena ordered champagne and we all had sips. Uncle Douglas was so sweet and gentle with Aunt Elena, and it seemed to me her eyes shone more when she was talking with him than with anybody else, and I felt sure deep in my heart that everything was going to work out with them just as I hoped it would. Grownups are often disappointing that way, but I was sure they wouldn't be.

Then it was time for us all to go to bed and we kissed everybody good night, and Mother and Daddy kissed Aunt Elena and thanked her and told her again how proud they were of her, and then Rob said sleepily, "Everybody's kissed Aunt Elena except Uncle Douglas."

Uncle Douglas said, "That will never do," and kissed her, and she looked even happier after that, and stood in the doorway waving and watching as we walked down the hall and around the corner to the elevator.

We slept late the next morning and had a nice, leisurely breakfast and then we set off for home. It seemed impossible that our vacation was completely over, and that so much had happened in just two short weeks, but it all had. We sang and sang on the way home, and suddenly we were in Clovenford. There was the road up the hill to the hospital, and there was the street that led to Daddy's office, and there was the railroad station. As we left the town and started up the hill to Thornhill we all stopped talking. Daddy just drove, and both Colette and Mr. Rochester sat braced and quivering with excitement but not moving. We passed the school and the church and the store, and then we were driving up our road, up our hill, and we saw our house, our own beautiful big rambly white house, and Daddy was pulling up to the garage, and we were home.

Home!

Our tongues and our muscles were suddenly freed and we piled out of the car and in through the garage and into the house, into the kitchen.

It was home and I remembered it with every bit of me, and yet in a funny way it was completely different. I can't quite explain. Sizes weren't the same. When I first looked at things they seemed smaller, and yet when I came back to them and looked at them again they seemed the same size they ought to be, and it would be as though we'd never been away at all.

Suzy had her arms full of cats and Colette was chasing Prunewhip and Mother was looking into the stove and the refrigerator and the cupboards and corners as though she had been away two months instead of two weeks.

And then we were all dashing all over the house to our special places. I ran up to Rob's and my room, and there was his little bed at the foot of my big one, and I would keep on sleeping there because Maggy wasn't being thrown to the lions, and the catalpa tree outside the east window was in full bloom and it had still been bare when we left for the island. I kept going from room to room, bumping into the others, and that's what we were all doing, feeling the feel of home again. Rochester was running up and down the stairs, up and down the stairs, thud, thud, thud, no longer grounded by a ladder he couldn't climb. And after she'd finished chasing Prunewhip, which she considered her natural duty, Colette curled up on her own green velvet cushion and went placidly to sleep.

We all ran outdoors (except Rochester, who was still practicing stairs) to the swing, to John and Dave's tree house, John, of course, to the barn to his space suit. We ran all the way around the house, looking at it from all four points of the compass, and then back into the house again, and Mother had music on the player, and the phone kept ringing, all the kids to ask us about our vacation, and the office phone, because Daddy's patients knew he was home again.

Rob grabbed my hand and pulled me back upstairs to our room and he said, "Oh, my bed, my own bed," and I knew his God Bless that night would go on for hours if someone didn't stop him from blessing every piece of furniture in the house and every tree outdoors.

Mother called us to help, and she was getting dinner and we realized that it *was* dinnertime and we were all starved, so we set the table and I mashed the potatoes and Suzy cut up the tomatoes for salad and Rob went around the table giving everyone three napkins. Then we were all around the table holding hands to say grace, and we said the kind of grace we always do on special occasions, each of us in turn saying our own, and when it came to Rob he said, "Oh, God, thank you for letting Maggy stay with us and making her not break so many of my toys any more, especially Elephant's Child, and thank you, God, for my good dinner, for the meat and mashed potatoes and gravy and 'sparagus, oh, no, God, I forgot, I don't like 'sparagus, and thank you for the milk and rolls and butter. Amen."

Of course, we couldn't help laughing, though Rob couldn't see that there was anything funny about it, and then everyone started to jabber all at once and to eat like pigs (though not Wilbur) and it all seemed right and comfortable and *home*. The office phone rang and Daddy answered it and said he had to go out for a few minutes but he wouldn't be long, and Mother said, "Now I know we're home again," and everybody laughed.

Maybe that's the best part of going away for a vacation— coming home again.

The L'Engle Cast

THE AUSTIN FAMILY
· · · · · · · · · · · ·

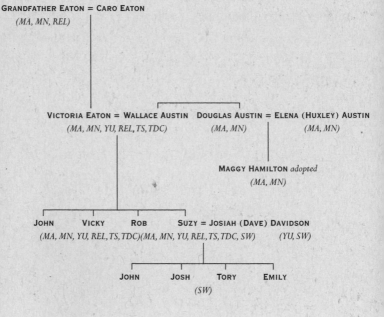

GRANDFATHER EATON = CARO EATON
(MA, MN, REL)

VICTORIA EATON = WALLACE AUSTIN   **DOUGLAS AUSTIN = ELENA (HUXLEY) AUSTIN**
(MA, MN, YU, REL, TS, TDC)   *(MA, MN)*   *(MA, MN)*

MAGGY HAMILTON *adopted*
(MA, MN)

JOHN   **VICKY**   **ROB**   **SUZY = JOSIAH (DAVE) DAVIDSON**
(MA, MN, YU, REL, TS, TDC)(MA, MN, YU, REL, TS, TDC, SW)   *(YU, SW)*

JOHN   **JOSH**   **TORY**   **EMILY**
(SW)

BOOKS FEATURING THE AUSTINS:

Meet the Austins *(MA)*   Troubling a Star *(TS)*
The Moon by Night *(MN)*   The Twenty-four Days
The Young Unicorns *(YU)*   Before Christmas *(TDC)*
A Ring of Endless Light *(REL)*   A Severed Wasp *(SW)*

# of Characters

THE MURRY-O'KEEFE FAMILY

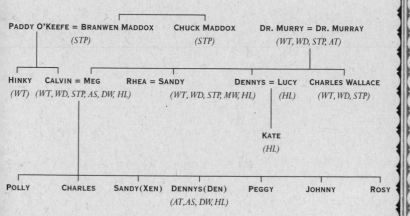

PADDY O'KEEFE = BRANWEN MADDOX   CHUCK MADDOX   DR. MURRY = DR. MURRAY
         (STP)   (STP)   (WT, WD, STP, AT)

HINKY   CALVIN = MEG   RHEA = SANDY   DENNYS = LUCY   CHARLES WALLACE
(WT)   (WT, WD, STP, AS, DW, HL)   (WT, WD, STP, MW, HL)   (HL)   (WT, WD, STP)

                                                      KATE
                                                      (HL)

POLLY   CHARLES   SANDY(XEN)   DENNYS(DEN)   PEGGY   JOHNNY   ROSY
                                   (AT, AS, DW, HL)

BOOKS FEATURING THE MURRY-O'KEEFES:

A Wrinkle in Time (WT)   An Acceptable Time (AT)
A Wind in the Door (WD)   The Arm of the Starfish (AS)
A Swiftly Tilting Planet (STP) Dragons in the Waters (DW)
Many Waters (MW)   A House Like Lotus (HL)

CHARACTERS WHO APPEAR IN BOTH SERIES:

CANON TALLIS (AS, YU, DW)   MR. THEOTOCOPOULOUS (YU, DW)
ADAM EDDINGTON (AS, REL, TS)   EMILY GREGORY (YU, DW, SW)
ZACHARY GRAY (MN, REL, AT, HL)

GOFISH

MADELEINE L'ENGLE

What did you want to be when you grew up?
A writer.

When did you realize you wanted to be a writer?
Right away. As soon as I was able to articulate, I knew I wanted to be a writer. And I read. I adored *Emily of New Moon* and some of the other L. M. Montgomery books and they impelled me because I loved them.

When did you start to write?
When I was five, I wrote a story about a little "gurl."

What was the first writing you had published?
When I was a child, a poem in *CHILD LIFE*. It was all about a lonely house and was very sentimental.

Where do you write your books?
Anywhere. I write in longhand first, and then type it.
My first typewriter was my father's pre–World War I
machine. It was the one he took with him to the war. It
had certainly been around the world.

**What is the best advice you have ever received
about writing?**
To just write.

What's your first childhood memory?
One early memory I have is going down to Florida for
a couple of weeks in the summertime to visit my
grandmother. The house was in the middle of a swamp,
surrounded by alligators. I don't like alligators, but there
they were, and I was afraid of them.

What is your favorite childhood memory?
Being in my room.

**As a young person, whom did you look up
to most?**
My mother. She was a storyteller and I loved her stories.
And she loved music and records. We played duets
together on the piano.

What was your worst subject in school?
Math and Latin. I didn't like the Latin teacher.

What was your best subject in school?
English.

What activities did you participate in at school?
I was president of the student government in boarding school and editor of a literary magazine, and also belonged to the drama club.

Are you a morning person or a night owl?
Night owl.

What was your first job?
Working for the actress Eva Le Gallienne, right after college.

What is your idea of the best meal ever?
Cream of Wheat. I eat it with a spoon. I love it with butter and brown sugar.

Which do you like better: cats or dogs?
I like them both. I once had a wonderful dog named Touché. She was a silver medium-sized poodle, and quite beautiful. I wasn't allowed to take her on the subway, and I couldn't afford to get a taxi, so I put her around my neck, like a stole. And she pretended she was a stole. She was an actor.

What do you value most in your friends?
Love.

What is your favorite song?
"Drink to Me Only with Thine Eyes."

What time of the year do you like best?
I suppose autumn. I love the changing of the leaves.
I love the autumn goldenrod, the Queen Anne's lace.

Which of your characters is most like you?
None of them. They're all wiser than I am.

Austin Family Chronicles

MEET THE AUSTINS

For a family with four kids, two dogs, assorted cats, and a constant stream of family and friends dropping by, life in the Austin family home has always been remarkably steady and contented. When a family friend suddenly dies, the Austins open their home to an orphaned girl, Maggy Hamilton. The Austin children—Vicky, John, Suzy, and Rob—do their best to be generous and welcoming to Maggy. Vicky knows she should feel sorry for Maggy, but having sympathy for Maggy is no easy thing. Maggy is moody and spoiled; she breaks toys, wakes people in the middle of the night screaming, discourages homework, and generally causes chaos in the Austin household. How can one small child disrupt a family of six? Will life ever return to normal?

978-0-312-37931-5, $6.99 US/$7.99 Can.

THE MOON BY NIGHT

As if simply being fourteen-years-old weren't bad enough—what with the usual teenage angst and uncertainty—Vicky Austin's always comforting and reliable home life is changing completely. Her brother John is going off to college in the fall. Maggy has gone to live with her legal guardian. And the rest of Vicky's family is moving from their quiet house in the country to the heart of New York City. But before the big move, the entire Austin family is taking a meandering trip across the country in their station wagon, stopping to camp along the way, with no set schedule and not a single night of camping experience among them. Wild animal attacks. Life-threatening natural disasters. Cute boys on the prowl. Anything can happen in the great outdoors.

978-0-312-37932-2, $6.99 US/$7.99 Can.

THE YOUNG UNICORNS

The Austins are trying to settle into their new life in New York City, but their once close-knit family is pulling away from each other. Their father spends long hours working alone in his study. John is away at college. Rob is making friends with people in the neighborhood: newspaper vendors, dog walkers, even the local rabbi. Suzy is blossoming into a vivacious young woman. And Vicky has become closer to Emily Gregory, a blind and brilliant young musician, than to her sister Suzy. With the Austins going in different directions, they don't notice that something sinister is going on in their neighborhood—and it's centered around them. A mysterious genie appears before Rob and Emily. A stranger approaches Vicky in the park and calls her by name. Members of a local gang are following their father. The entire Austin family is in danger. If they don't start telling each other what's going on, someone just might get killed.

978-0-312-37933-9, $6.99 US/$7.99 Can.

A RING OF ENDLESS LIGHT

After a tumultuous year in New York City, the Austins are spending the summer on the small island where their grandfather lives. He's very sick, and watching his condition deteriorate as the summer passes is almost more than Vicky can bear. To complicate matters, she finds herself as the center of attention for three very different boys. Zachary Gray, the troubled and reckless boy Vicky met last summer, wants her all to himself as he grieves the loss of his mother. Leo Rodney has been just a friend for years, but the tragic loss of his father causes him to turn to Vicky for comfort—and romance. And then there's Adam Eddington. Adam is only asking Vicky to help with his research on dolphins. But Adam—and the dolphins—may just be what Vicky needs to get through this heartbreaking summer.

978-0-312-37935-3, $6.99 US/$7.99 Can.

TROUBLING A STAR

The Austins have settled back into their beloved home in the country after more than a year away. Though they had all missed the predictability and security of life in Thornhill, Vicky Austin is discovering that slipping back into her old life isn't easy. She's been changed by life in New York City and her travels around the country while her old friends seem to have stayed the same. So Vicky finds herself spending time with a new friend, Serena Eddington—the great-aunt of a boy Vicky met over the summer. Aunt Serena gives Vicky an incredible birthday gift—a month-long trip to Antarctica. It's the opportunity of a lifetime. But Vicky is nervous. She's never been away from her family before. Once she sets off though, she finds that's the least of her worries. She receives threatening letters. She's surrounded by suspicious characters. Vicky no longer knows who to trust. And she may not make it home alive.

978-0-312-37934-6, $6.99 US/$7.99 Can.

ALSO AVAILABLE:

A Wrinkle in Time, 978-0-312-36754-1
A Wind in the Door, 978-0-312-36854-8
A Swiftly Tilting Planet, 978-0-312-36856-2
Many Waters, 978-0-312-36857-9
An Acceptable Time, 978-0-312-36858-6

SQUARE
FISH

Available at your local bookstore, or visit
www.squarefishbooks.com.